This Little Family

This Little Family

:

Inès Bayard

translated from the French by Adriana Hunter

OTHER PRESS / NEW YORK

Copyright © Éditions Albin Michel, 2018
Originally published in French as *Le malheur du bas* in 2018
by Éditions Albin Michel, Paris
English translation copyright © Other Press, 2020

Epigraph from *Things* by Georges Perec. Copyright © René Julliard, 1965.
Translated from the French by David Bellos.
Translation copyright © William Collins Sons & Co. Ltd, 1990.

Quote on page 117 from *Lust* by Elfriede Jelinek,
translated by Michael Hulse (NY: Serpent's Tail, 1992).

Production editor: Yvonne E. Cárdenas
Text designer: Jennifer Daddio / Bookmark Design & Media Inc.
This book was set in Stempel Schneidler by
Alpha Design & Composition of Pittsfield, NH.

1 3 5 7 9 10 8 6 4 2

Library of Congress Cataloging-in-Publication Data

Names: Bayard, Inès, 1992- author. | Hunter, Adriana, translator.
Title: This little family : a novel / Inès Bayard ; translated from
the French by Adriana Hunter.
Other titles: Malheur du bas. English
Description: New York : Other Press, [2020]
Identifiers: LCCN 2019056816 (print) | LCCN 2019056817 (ebook) |
ISBN 9781892746870 (paperback) | ISBN 9781892746672 (ebook)
Classification: LCC PQ2702.A968 M3513 2020 (print) |
LCC PQ2702.A968 (ebook) | DDC 843/.92—dc23
LC record available at https://lccn.loc.gov/2019056816
LC ebook record available at https://lccn.loc.gov/2019056817

To
Geneviève Combas Boteilla

You cannot live in a frenzy for very long.

In a world which promised so much

and delivered nothing,

the tension was too great.

—GEORGES PEREC, *THINGS*

∶

Little Thomas didn't have time to finish his stewed apple. His mother hadn't given him the slightest chance. The speed with which the poison circulated through his blood simply meant he didn't suffer when he died. Only Marie's body was still upright, securely wedged against the back of her chair, her head tipped back. She must have struggled to ensure this was noticed. Laurent had been served first. Few people stumbling across these three ashen bodies could have imagined the warm laughter filling the room just moments before the tragedy occurred.

Marie felt absolutely no remorse and, apart from her final gesture, there was no sign of a struggle. Every object was in its usual place, the strong flavorsome smell of the meal still hung in the air in the kitchen, paper napkins hardly marked, a water jug placed squarely in the middle of the table. The child was still in his booster seat, his face pitched forward onto his plate and the last morsels he hadn't wanted to eat. His dimpled little fingers hung limply. Marie's fists, meanwhile, rested squarely on the table. There had been only one tragic event in her life, but one powerful enough to goad her to action. Her face looked peaceful, at last. Her features relaxed, her body utterly freed of all pointless suffering. She had finally become the woman in the picture, the sort of woman who succeeds in controlling her own destiny.

Her husband had suffered terribly. He'd felt his lungs fill with blood, his breathing slow, and his throat constrict as his moist flesh convulsed. He had fallen from his chair and crawled for many a long minute, spitting liters of blood and vomit over the kitchen's white-tiled floor. But he wasn't dead. He was the only survivor, and was hastily evacuated a few hours later, still hovering between life and death. In the first seconds of this hellish chaos, his wife, who hadn't yet touched her own food, had watched him slump to the floor before giving the first poisoned mouthfuls to her son. She hadn't wanted gushing blood. There'd been enough blood already. Poisoning had struck her as the most judicious option. Laurent's cell had kept vibrating on the console table in the hall. Perhaps he might have found out the truth before taking his first taste.

The Charonne district was cordoned off by the police. Just a precaution. The investigators soon grasped what she'd done. The two corpses were extricated from their chairs. The stiffness in their limbs meant the medical examiner had to relax them by injection before sealing them in body bags under the stunned gaze of their neighbors across the landing.

Marie had contemplated killing her son before, several times and in different ways. She was very determined. Day after day, the false innocence in the child's eyes had driven her to murder. But until now, circumstances had stopped her seeing it through, mostly for practical reasons. She had killed her little boy and it was simply justice being done.

Before any revelations that might invite the first verdicts, let's take a moment to appreciate the figure of this dead woman surrounded by her loved ones, the only one of the three to have remained upright.

⋮

As on every Monday, Marie will arrive at work five minutes late. She's known for six years that this will never change. It has simply become another part of her daily routine. Laurent is fussing in the kitchen, nursing a lukewarm cup of coffee. Marie watches him just as tenderly as she did ten years ago. Things weren't so different back then. They met at a student party organized by a mutual friend. Marie was a shy, reserved young woman and didn't immediately respond to Laurent's advances. It took considerable perseverance on his part before she granted him a first date. They were married three years later in Bois-le-Roi, with the affectionate support of both of their families and their friends.

From the very start theirs was a straightforward happiness, their love enough to give each of them more than him- or herself to think about. She takes care of him, encourages his plans, reassures him when he doubts himself, and helps him find his files every morning so he isn't late for work. Laurent's love for Marie is genuine and deep, but he is not as attentive to her as she to him. They're not a couple who instantly understand each other. They need to discuss, expand, explain. Four years ago, Laurent was taken on by a big law firm that specializes in probate and divorce. His workday begins at nine and often goes on till late. Marie understands his ambition and does not judge him for it. She earns less than he does but enjoys her job at the bank. When she arrives at the branch on the place de la République in the morning, she feels useful and enjoys her commitment to helping other people, giving them advice and suggesting options to them. Money has never stirred her to great plans, but she's happy that she and Laurent have a comfortable life.

Shortly after they were married, Laurent and Marie decided to move to a large apartment on the boulevard Voltaire in the Eleventh Arrondissement of Paris. They were immediately taken with the neighborhood's friendly atmosphere. The arcades that run from the place de la Nation up to the place de la République are filled with little shops and businesses, at lunchtime their apartment is often pervaded by the smell of chicken from the local rotisserie, and on Sundays they can hear the bell ring on buses that stop at every crossroad through the busy bustling market. They've always loved Paris, and over the years have accumulated a good many friends and developed a varied, interesting social life. Laurent moves in more sophisticated circles than Marie. Thanks to a highly publicized divorce case between a former soccer star and a well-loved actress, he has already forged himself a solid reputation in certain journalistic circles. He and Marie are frequently invited to private parties where intellectual Paris rubs shoulders with business Paris. Marie never feels awkward. She's proud to be there with her husband and makes the most of her own discreet charms to captivate those around him. Immersed in the contentment of her day-to-day existence, she quietly ensures everything is under control without drawing any attention to the fact. She is the one who runs the household. Her upbringing and her parents' unconditional love protected her from the boundless torments of childhood and adolescence. Of course, she has often had to confront complex or difficult situations, but she has never for a moment felt she was losing her grip on her life.

The fall is Marie's favorite time of year. A poetic season. The plane trees on the boulevard Voltaire are dropping their orangey leaves on the sidewalk, the air is cool but mostly dry, and the sky azure blue. Sunbeams light up part of the kitchen. Marie gazes serenely out the window. "Look how pretty it is! Did you see all these colors?" Laurent doesn't reply. He's frantically looking for his file from yesterday. Marie smiles when she sees that it's staring right at him on the kitchen counter. She steps over to hand it to him, a knowing smile on her lips. Laurent looks at her, amused, then kisses her before racing out to work. Marie finds routine reassuring. She knows what she needs to do before even thinking about it, and although some might feel disenfranchised by this, it has never bothered her. Marie finishes her coffee and leaves at eight forty-five.

Almost before she is in the street she can feel the morning hustle, the whirl of France at work, keeping it together. Marie acknowledges that she's never had to struggle to make ends meet. Born into a middle-class family with traditional values, pampered at every turn, encouraged and steered by her parents in her every choice, she is in no position to understand how people get into a downward spiral. It's not that she lacks compassion. She often puts herself in someone else's position, in her clients', for example, to understand what's really at stake in their lives, what their risks are, what they stand to gain or lose.

As she emerges from the République Métro station she has only a few minutes' walk to reach the bank at

9:05. Her coworkers are always friendly, greeting her with a smile, offering her a coffee before her meetings and asking for her well-considered opinion. Marie is a financial consultant, a privileged position, well up in the bank's hierarchy. Her clients like her very much and her drawers are filled with all sorts of gifts: boxes of chocolates, bottles of wine, homemade preserves, scarves…When she arrives home from work in the evening, Marie likes to tell her husband about the day's amusing little events or the disagreements she occasionally needs to address. Money lies at the heart of everything in her work. Her standard clients are people with enough income to contemplate lucrative investments. On Monday mornings Marie always has to check her best clients' accounts to familiarize herself with any new transactions. On her huge desk there are framed photographs of Laurent and herself on vacation, her family, her sister and her nephew, and her late grandmother. It suddenly occurs to her that she doesn't see enough of her family. Since she was born her parents have lived in a large house in Bois-le-Roi, just a few miles from Paris. Her sister lives with her husband and son in the Ninth Arrondissement, in the Saint-Georges neighborhood. The sisters are very close and are due to have lunch together today.

Her telephone starts to ring. Monsieur Collard doesn't understand why a payment he asked to have made has still not gone through; Madame Siris would like to know whether she can use the money from her life insurance to give her son a new car for his birthday; Madame Frousard wonders whether her husband will still agree to pay her the lump sum he promised when they divorced. Each client has a problem, and Marie knows exactly how to solve it. The hours spool by, meetings come one after the other. In the distance there is chanting from demonstrations against a law allowing homosexuals to marry, it reverberates all over Paris. Through her office window, Marie watches hundreds of thousands of people tramping the streets and brandishing enormous pink-and-blue banners around the place de la République. Her parents told her they considered joining the demonstration but in the end they weren't able to reach the location in time. Laurent is against this law too. Like many French children, Laurent and Marie were baptized, went to Bible study classes, and occasionally attended Mass with their parents on Sunday mornings or for religious festivals. Marie feels that this law is a question of religion and principle. "Well, they're right, aren't they?" her client exclaims. "Marriage is for a man and a woman, it always has been. Even some homosexuals are against this law." Marie looks at her client and smiles. She thinks her comment vapid but is more comfortable concentrating on the woman's home insurance contract.

It's lunchtime. Marie slips out of the office to join her sister Roxane in a brasserie on the rue de Bretagne. All the streets that lead to the place de la République are still barricaded by the police. When they watched the news last night, Laurent admitted he was finding it increasingly difficult to cope with the endless demonstrations in Paris. Marie, on the other hand, finds it refreshing. She certainly won't participate in any sort of protest movement but is happy other people do it for her.

Roxane is sitting at an outside table with her baby in his buggy. It's her day off. Marie is happy to see her, kisses her and sits next to her. The child whimpers a little before Roxane gives him his bottle. Marie watches him fondly, strokes him, and showers him with affectionate pet names. Roxane tells her about her recent holiday with Julien in Rome. While they were away, the baby went to his grandparents, who couldn't wait to look after him. Everyone in the family wants to know what Laurent and Marie are waiting for before having their first child. She is thirty-one, he thirty-three. There couldn't be a better time to start a family. She just hasn't had the opportunity to think about it. Their respective careers needed a while to take shape and so far their ambitions have been focused on work. "Watch out, you'll be too old soon! You don't want them calling you Grandma!" Roxane had her first child at twenty-four. She looks happy but tired. Yes, people talk about the tiredness but they don't make a big thing of it. The joys of parenthood are enough to make other people understand that they too should throw themselves into the adventure. An hour has gone by. Marie and Roxane leave the restaurant and say goodbye with a long hug, promising they'll call each other very soon.

It's the end of the day. The sun is only just starting to set. Marie walks up the rue du Temple to buy a few things at the Monoprix supermarket. She'd like to cook something nice for Laurent this evening, there might be time to make a blanquette of veal. The autumn wind is pleasantly bracing on her face. People hurry through shop entrances. No one seems to dawdle in any one place, as if everyone has made a deliberate effort to go in different directions. There's no such thing as stasis in Paris. She collects her bicycle, which she left near the bank yesterday because of the rain, puts her shopping in the small basket at the front, and sets off toward boulevard Voltaire.

Laurent isn't home yet so she has a couple of hours left to prepare the meal. She knows he'll be very happy to have his favorite dish when he comes home. As she peels the vegetables on the kitchen counter Marie thinks over what her sister said at lunchtime.

She contemplates motherhood. As a child she already knew she'd be a mother and spent hours looking after the baby dolls her parents gave her for Christmas. She now feels ready to have a baby with Laurent, and maybe that's why she thought of making this particular dish this evening. She'd like to stop taking the pill and start a family.

It's eight thirty, time seems to be going so quickly. The blanquette is simmering and the table's set. Marie recognizes Laurent's ritual as he comes through the door. He lobs his keys onto the sideboard in the hall, hangs his coat on the hook, takes three steps before realizing he hasn't closed the door, closes it, then calls her name—"Marie!"—to check that she's there.

She can tell from his smile and how quickly he moves that he has good news to tell her. "I got the Lancarde case!" he announces. She's thrilled and throws her arms around him to congratulate him. They hug tenderly, kiss, and look into each other's eyes. He lifts her up, sits her gently on the sideboard, and kisses her again. Gérard Lancarde is a wealthy industrialist who specializes in the plastics market in Europe. His father, who founded the Calcum consortium fifty years ago, was meant to hand over more than half the ventures within the company when he officially took retirement. Except that a few years before the cession he married a Russian singer with a huge following in her own country, and, against his son's advice, bequeathed to her a substantial proportion of his shares. Laurent is still reeling from receiving the news himself. "I don't know if you have any idea, honey. This contract deals with an inheritance worth hundreds of millions of euros and he chose me, personally! I can't believe it." Marie is genuinely happy for him. Laurent goes over to the still-steaming casserole dish and she watches him affectionately, his childish pleasure, the way he slowly lifts the lid and closes his eyes as he smells the meat. But she suddenly remembers wanting a baby. With this new contract maybe Laurent won't have time for that. A slight cramping feeling ripples through her stomach.

After explaining his new case in detail for an hour, Laurent doesn't seem to have noticed her turmoil at all.

"You know I saw my sister today, darling. That little Guillaume is so adorable. Wait till you see him, he's grown again!" Laurent is receptive but makes no connection with their own circumstances and keeps eating. Confronted with this dead end, Marie decides to state her case openly. "I want a baby. I think it's the right time, I think we can start our family now. I can feel it, I'm ready."

Laurent lets a piece of veal fall from his mouth. He's stunned by the news, his face drains of color. It hadn't occurred to him. Or he hadn't had time to think about it, at least. Silence settles over the room. Marie holds her breath, waiting for his reply before she can breathe again. Laurent smiles, gets up from his chair and kisses her full on the mouth. "My darling. I want to! Of course I want to have a baby with you!" Marie's body relaxes, flooded with intense relief and happiness. She thinks she's never felt so weightless, every corner of her being is intoxicated, blissfully shaking off all tension. She feels like screaming from the rooftops of Paris, calling her parents, her sister, her colleagues and clients to tell them the big news before she's even pregnant.

After their blanquette of veal this evening, Laurent and Marie will lie in bed arm in arm, pressed up close in the elation of their plans.

．
．
．

The decision to have a baby with Laurent has put Marie in a permanent good mood. As she pedals along the boulevard du Temple she has a sudden realization how very lucky she is to be this person. She loves her work, lives with a husband she adores, wants for nothing, and will soon be welcoming her first child into the world. She can picture family meals at Bois-le-Roi with Laurent and the baby. The new photos she'll be able to put on her desk and show off to her clients. The long walks in the Luxembourg Gardens, the pride she'll feel pushing her buggy toward the large central pond. She'll be a loving, attentive mother like her own mother. All at once she notices she's seeing more children than usual.

There's a constant to-and-fro of buggies and little figures everywhere around her. Hurrying and alert, mothers resolutely perform the first stage of their marathon: taking their children to school, kissing them goodbye, and waiting to check that they get inside the building.

Marie arrives at the bank on time. She knows that this Tuesday will be harder than usual because there's the quarterly sales results meeting. She's not a very good salesperson and during these committee meetings her immediate boss always opts to praise her understanding and analytical abilities rather than her head for business. This afternoon she'll be introduced to the Paris-based company's new CEO for the Tenth Arrondissement. He's made a point of attending such meetings to encourage his teams. Everyone at the bank is fretting at the thought of being reprimanded for poor results.

Hervé, the other asset management adviser, is particularly anxious. He knows he hasn't made the grade during this first trimester and Marie feels bad for him. She can tell that this man, pushing fifty and coming toward the end of his career, is especially despondent about his work, his clients, and the pace imposed by the company's new diktats. He'd like to give up but has no choice. He needs to pay the mortgage, provide pocket money for his thankless teenage daughter, support the wife with whom he hasn't been able to picture a loving future for years, and keep a little money for his passion, ornithology. Hervé is fascinated by wild pigeon species, turtledoves in particular. In a drawer of his desk he keeps a secret file of all the articles he's found on the subject. He's very proud of it. After a difficult appointment with a client or sometimes simply for the pleasure of it, he takes out his file and spends the rare moments of peace in his life leafing through these yellowed photographs of birds gliding through the air. Hervé is endearing but deeply unhappy.

Marie sits herself at the meeting table, laden with a pile of files that she hopes will be adequate in her defense. There's a deathly silence in the large room except for the crackling of a fluorescent light with a loose connection. The branch manager gets up to switch it off. Marie has always been awed by her crisp manner and authoritative stride. When the two of them are alone in her office, Marie keeps her head down, trying to avoid eye contact. Colette Sirmont is a strong, willful, demanding, and almost oppressive career woman. Marie sees nothing of herself in any of her characteristics, either in her professional or her personal life. When Marie has meetings with her clients alone she's relaxed, at her ease, and sometimes even surprisingly amusing. Her work at the bank allows her to play the part of someone else. With Laurent she can't seem to establish her identity as anything other than gentle and restrained, just as she already was with him and his friends ten years ago. All around the room people eye their coworkers, studying them in an effort to determine who's in the worst position.

The CEO arrives and slams the door. Faces screw up, hands don't know where to put themselves, throats constrict politely. He's tall, imposing, a rather attractive man. The women have noticed. With the sharp eyes of someone accustomed to managing other people, he quickly takes up his position at the head of the table. And is happier staying on his feet.

Marie watches him from afar. While his assistant starts up the overhead projector, he begins his talk, saying that he won't have time to discuss things case by case and would prefer to analyze individual results in one-on-one meetings over the coming week. There's a ripple of relief around the room. Marie is asked to speak about her experience selling the new life insurance package. She stands up, eyes lowered, and walks over to join the CEO. He stares at her intently, appraising her. Marie can smell his scent. A powerful combination of eau de cologne, leather, and sandalwood. She never wears perfume, Laurent doesn't like it. When Marie has finished her report she walks back to her seat, under the satisfied gaze of the CEO. A coworker congratulates her, saying she argued her case well for her marketing methods. After an hour the CEO brings the meeting to a close and everyone leaves the room to return to work. Hervé is relieved but he knows it won't last and that he has only a few days' respite before receiving his sentence. As she leaves, Marie catches the CEO's eye, and he smiles and nods at her. She has three more meetings this afternoon. She gets on with her day.

It's six thirty. Marie has finished helping the day's clients understand financial codes of practice and can leave at last. Once outside, she finds to her surprise that she still has that effervescent feeling. She's so calm, level, moderate, and patient, Paris gives her a buzz, brings her alive. She always felt slightly wrong living out of town as a teenager. Granted, Bois-le-Roi isn't far from Paris, but she was frustrated by the journey she had to make on the *transilien* train every weekend to meet up with her friends in the city. She always knew she'd live in Paris later.

The October night is closing in and she thinks the rue Meslay feels darker than usual, perhaps one of the streetlights isn't working. Marie doesn't remember exactly where she left her bike. Maybe outside the little Turkish restaurant where she likes to have lunch on Thursdays. The street is as good as deserted, with just a few pedestrians hurrying home. The tall buildings are lit up with warm lights. She's always liked looking into apartment windows when she walks through the city's streets. Discovering people's intimate lives, their taste in interior design, seeing children playing and parents chatting on the balcony or cooking. She suddenly wonders whether other people do this too, whether anyone watches her walking around her apartment. Under the weak glow of the streetlights she can make out her bicycle in the distance. It's tipped onto the ground, the front wheel horribly twisted, one tire gone, and the frame broken. Horrified, she runs over, tries pointlessly to stand it back up against the pillar, but quickly realizes she won't be able to ride it. She feels helpless. This is the first time in her life she's been the victim of an act of vandalism. She casts around for some form of help and reaches into her bag for her cell to call Laurent. She knows that he won't come over for such a small thing and is bound to tell her to catch the Métro home, but she needs to hear his voice, to be reassured. He picks up on the second ring.

"You'll never believe this, someone tried to steal my bike. I don't even have a front wheel now, they trashed the whole thing." Laurent is on edge, he's about to go into a meeting to set up Gérard Lancarde's defense. He tells her to take the Métro and leave her bike where it is. While she's still talking to Laurent she notices a familiar-looking silhouette on the same sidewalk as she is. The company's CEO recognizes her.

"Well, well, what happened to you?" Marie hangs up. She's slightly ashamed, feels stupid with her beaten-up bike. She explains the situation, doing her best to disguise her distress. The CEO smiles and tries to calm her with a friendly pat on the shoulder. "Look, my car isn't far at all. I could drive you home if you like. Where do you live?" Marie looks at him for a moment, embarrassed. Then, not keen to take the Métro, which will be packed with rush-hour commuters, she decides to accept his offer.

On the way to his car they fall in step together, the clipped rhythm of their footfalls resonating on the sidewalk. He hardly says a word but smiles at her from time to time, turning to face her. She's awed by him. He's the CEO. He takes his car keys from his coat to open the Mercedes that's perfectly parked by the curb. The headlights flash. He seems somehow proud of this flourish while still careful to remain strangely modest. Marie settles into the passenger seat. The smell of leather mingles with a strong blast of the scent she smelled on him during the afternoon's meeting. He throws his coat onto the rear seat and then sits down and starts up the car; the engine purrs. Marie is relieved it's not a very long journey. Her phone chimes in her bag. It's a message from Laurent, asking if everything's okay. He'll be home late because he's agreed to have dinner with his client, and tells her not to wait up.

Marie's disappointed, she would have liked him to be with her this evening to comfort her.

The CEO turns on the radio and Marie recognizes the opening notes of Erik Satie's Third Gnossienne, her father's favorite. In an instant this composition with its ambiguous melodies darkens her interpretation of Paris. The darkness feels stifling, the heady smell of sandalwood and the lights reflecting on the windshield giddying. The end of boulevard Voltaire appears at last. The man doesn't move a muscle, his hands clamped firmly to the steering wheel, his eyes staring ahead, his lips motionless. She doesn't dare turn to look at him. Time slows, freezes, chokes the space. Everything stagnates. She wants to get out. A car stops on a level with them at a red light and a woman smiles at her briefly before looking away. The car sets off again. There are only a few buildings left before they reach her apartment but there are no parking spaces and the boulevard is full of traffic. Marie wants to be let off onto the street but he chooses instead to drive around into rue Richard-Lenoir to find a better place. "This city really is impossible for cars."

Marie feels the engine slow at last and the radio snaps off. They now enter a private car park where he pulls into a space. Silence settles into the darkness, against which she can make out the man's tall silhouette. There are no passersby. "Thank you so much for driving me home, it was very kind of you. I mean, you really didn't have to. I'm sorry but I need to go now, my husband's expecting me and he'll be worried." She doesn't know exactly why she came up with this lie. A subtle discomfort grips her stomach like the protracted suspense a viewer feels watching a film, before everything becomes clear at the end.

"Wouldn't you like to stay here with me for a while?" the man asks, still looking dead ahead, his hands resting loosely on the steering wheel.

Marie starts to feel the first inklings of panic. She curses whoever destroyed her bike this evening, cornering her in this uncomfortable situation. "I really think you should stay awhile," he insists. Marie hears the sudden clunk of the lock on her door. He's locking her in. His shadow—an imposing, frightening presence—moves slowly closer, approaching her with implied intimacy. She feels something cold and smooth slide over her thighs. A shudder runs through her whole body, which is still secured to the seat by her seat belt. She struggles and asks him firmly to stop and let her out. She wants to scream but, strangely, doesn't dare to. She wonders why this is...Maybe she doesn't want to disturb the whole neighborhood, draw attention to herself for nothing. She doesn't want to embarrass herself in front of her CEO for seeing an assault in what might simply be a rather clumsy attempt at seduction.

He anticipates her every reaction and swiftly flattens one hand over her mouth while his other hand insinuates itself inside her blouse and works progressively down toward her panties. He drives his fingers inside her. Marie's body shakes, sweating from every pore, her flesh frozen into the thick leather of her seat. She starts to fight, pushing against his chest that's pinning her down. He's too strong, much too strong. She now knows she won't be able to escape. Marie is going to be raped here in this car. Like those women on TV who describe how they were attacked, she'll have to go through that too. She struggles with all her might. Her wrists are bruised, her legs pinioned, her voice silenced, her stomach crushed. She can hear the man's moans, his little gasps of pleasure in the crook of her neck. He unhooks her seat belt and presses firmly on the lever to lower her backrest. She jolts down and back. He spreads himself over her, mounts onto her. Marie can feel his erection through his pants. She keeps fighting, screaming. No one will hear. Her thin arms are gripped by just one of the man's hands while his other hand labors to undo his belt and the fly buttons on his suit. She feels her cell phone fall onto the car floor mat, vibrating and ringing under her feet, and is overwhelmed with frustration that she can't reach it. The silk panties that Laurent bought her for Valentine's Day last year are torn in a fraction of a second. He scratches her at the same time. One last surge of energy convulses her, twisting her body in every direction, her feet stretching as far as they can to get away from him. She's very soon exhausted, drained of strength. All her limbs ache for failing to help her. He penetrates her. The to-and-fro starts up, slowly at first, then harder. It hurts. Her vagina is dry, its walls rasped until they bleed. She remembers the slight burning sensations she had a few years ago because of genital herpes, and how much that hurt.

The man suddenly stops. With a single confident hand he grabs her hair and forces her over onto her stomach. Marie hears him mutter a few words, but can't give the sounds any meaning. Reality distorts, nothing exists anymore. She's going to wake up. Maybe she's just in the bank's staff rest area. Maybe her mind misinterpreted the look the man gave her before he left the meeting. She's fallen asleep. Hervé's going to wake her. His penis is hard as a weapon. He strikes deep inside her belly with violent thrusts. The pain makes her throw up over the rear seat. He doesn't stop. His breathing accelerates. "Come here!" he says, lifting his heavy body toward Marie's face. His hard penis hovers expectantly under her mouth. "Go on, put it in your mouth." She twists her head in every direction, begs him to stop, tries to free herself from his hold. He stills her face with his hands, and his knees restrict her movements, then he rams his penis into her mouth, right to the back of her throat. It smells slightly of urine. She's going to choke. She bites into it with her teeth. He pulls out and slaps her. "Filthy bitch! So that's what you want!" He still has an erection. He comes back into her from behind, sodomizing her. She's never done this with anyone. Marie can feel liquid trickling over her legs. The pain is intolerable. He switches back to her vagina and eventually comes inside her with a groan of pleasure. It's over. His penis is limp, soaked in semen, vomit, blood, excrement, and vaginal fluid. He's satisfied and clambers furtively back to his seat to button up his pants. "That's it, you can go."

Marie sits up painfully, her body burning, swollen, weighed down with the agony of her slack muscles and her taut compressed skin. The locks click open. She steps out of the car, her slacks still hanging down over the tops of her thighs. He grabs her arm firmly and pulls her back onto the seat. "If you talk to anyone about what happened, you, your husband and your career are all finished. No one'll believe you, so you keep your mouth shut and everything can go on like before." In the feeble yellow glow of a streetlight Marie surreptitiously notices the gleam of a wedding ring on the man's finger. The car engine starts up. She climbs out and stumbles a few steps out of the car park. The door slams behind her and the car pulls away.

Marie doesn't tell herself it's over. She knows this is just the beginning. The entrance to her building is a little farther up the street, on the corner of the boulevard Voltaire. It's not quite eight o'clock; Laurent is most likely having his dinner. He must have been on the way to the restaurant, joshing with his coworkers and his new client while his wife was being raped by her boss, penetrated in every orifice on the seat of a car. She goes into the building and meets the caretaker wheeling out the trash cans. "Hello, Madame Campan, how are you?" Marie keeps her head down and slips away into the shadows in the corridor, answering with "A little tired, but I'm fine! Good night" as she goes up in the elevator. She hopes he didn't notice anything unusual. She knows already that she's in the process of hiding the evil event, that she won't say anything, that no one will ever know about the assault.

The apartment is shrouded in darkness partially diluted by the open curtains allowing light from the boulevard into the living room. There's no one there. She'd like to call her husband to reassure him. Every step toward the kitchen is painful. The central corridor that leads to all the rooms in the apartment seems never-ending, almost ridiculous. She picks up the handset that she left on the sideboard this morning and dials Laurent's number. She hopes he doesn't pick up so she can leave a controlled message with no fluctuations or lurching in her breathing. He doesn't answer. "Yes, it's me. So I finally got home, one of the Métro lines was blocked...I'm going to take a shower and go to bed, I'm exhausted. I hope everything's going well with your client. I love you."

She hangs up, feeling absent, empty. She thinks this is best, and anyway, if she wanted to admit anything to him she wouldn't find the right way to do it. He would always look at her differently, not only as his wife but as the victim, the woman who was raped, sodomized for the first time by another penis than his. Marie is suddenly aware of the smell of vomit on her. She doesn't have the strength to take a shower but she still needs to. If she were single she would just take some sleeping pills and go to bed, but if she doesn't wash now Laurent will notice this aftershave that isn't his on his wife's body, the sheets will be impregnated with the smell, and everything will fall apart all over again.

Standing in the middle of the bathroom she slowly unbuttons her blouse and painfully lowers her slacks with the shreds of her torn panties still clinging to them. Blood has dried on her thighs. Foul-smelling brownish marks trail over her stomach. Now completely naked, she catches her reflection in the mirror above the basin. She moves closer and makes out traces of dried semen at the corner of her mouth. One eye is slightly swollen where he slapped her, but that will almost certainly have disappeared by tomorrow. This vision of herself floods her with unbounded sadness. The anger is sure to come later. The scalding water runs between her breasts, washes over her stomach, flows down the nape of her neck and relaxes her muscles. She collapses against the wall, hunches over, limply holding the showerhead above her. Everything she does becomes an ordeal, as if she's never previously noticed how difficult it is to perform on a daily basis—stepping out of the shower, wrapping herself in a towel, putting on her pajamas. She knows she won't be able to get to sleep tonight, nor perhaps for days to come. She needs sleeping pills, but in a flash it comes back to her: after Laurent had a bad reaction to a drug past its use-by date, she decided to have a clean-out. She clearly remembers throwing out the last sleeping tablets. The clock in the corridor says it's ten o'clock. The pharmacy will be closed and she would never be able to go out again anyway.

The bedroom is a mess. Laurent was looking all over the apartment for his files again this morning and he thought that maybe they were hiding under the sheets. Everything is upside down. Marie never berates him for anything but right now a diffuse anger spreads through her whole body. She was raped this evening, assaulted, attacked, and she can't even have sleeping pills or her husband by her side or a tidy bed. She buries herself under the cold sheets, turns out the small bedside light, and waits with her eyes open for sleep to be so good as to take her.

She thinks it's about midnight when she hears Laurent come home. She recognizes his footsteps, his stride, his rhythm. From the way he lumbers around the hall she can tell he's had a little too much to drink. That's good, he's sure to sleep. Every creak of the wooden floor stresses her. She wishes she could open the windows and jump into thin air before her husband reaches the bedroom. He sidles up close to her, his body hot and naked. "Are you asleep, honey?" She immediately closes her eyes, relaxes the muscles of her face, slightly slows her breathing and gives a few soft grunts. Laurent eventually turns away. His body rolls to the other side of the bed, far away from her. He's a happy, healthy, well-fed man full of drink and plans for the future, he can fall asleep in a matter of minutes. His wife on the other hand knows she'll have to pretend to live and sleep for many days to come. Marie opens her eyes. The silence is interrupted by the sound of scooters on the boulevard. Her eyes don't move, staring straight ahead. Deep in the night, facing the wall that she's previously looked at while bowled over by pleasure, the trouble down below feels to her like fate's revenge on a life it deems too easy.

.
.
.

Marie got up several times in the night; Laurent didn't notice a thing. She thought he'd be very tired this morning after his long evening but he clearly isn't. She watches in silence as he paces around the kitchen. "I'm sure I put it here when I came home." Marie doesn't react. "I'll end up putting tracking devices on all my files so I can find them. I'm super-late!" Marie can't remember a single day when she hasn't helped him find his stuff. Her husband notices something different this morning. "You okay, honey? You seem miles away." She spots Laurent's green folder on the fruit dish. She doesn't tell him, waits for him to fret a little as he watches the minutes trickle by. She's just about to tell him when he sees it. "Ah, there it is. I knew it was in the kitchen! Okay, I'm off to work, Jean's waiting for me. And don't forget we're going to Paul and Sophia's for dinner this evening. They're expecting us at eight. Love you!" He drops his cup in the sink, kisses his wife, and runs out of the kitchen.

Obviously, Marie had forgotten this dinner. The stigmata of last night's attack materialize again. Her vagina hurts, it's burning and painfully swollen. All her joints are stiff, her knees and wrists ache. Maybe she should see a doctor. It's eight thirty, time to go to work.

When she's downstairs she looks for her bicycle in the building's small inner courtyard. Gripped with sudden panic, she rings the caretaker's doorbell. "Hi, sorry to disturb you, but did you see my bicycle?" As she asks the question she remembers: the remains of her bike are still at République. And then she was raped. She backs away slowly. "I'm so sorry, I remember now. I left it at work." The caretaker smiles at her, thinking she must be working too hard and is tired this morning.

The day seems to go on forever. She wishes she could slip away and lie down, sleep for a lifetime. She sits facing her elderly customer with a rigid smile on her face. And yet the woman is promising a handsome investment, more than three hundred thousand euros of life insurance. With this contract Marie could make her grand entrance into the top three of the sales team for this quarter. Her coworkers will be full of admiration and the CEO will congratulate her personally. He raped her yesterday evening. Marie can't stay upright on her chair any longer. Her lower back hurts, the pain in her vagina is radiating up to her stomach, wracking her guts with sharp spasms, swelling and subsiding, making it difficult for her to concentrate. "Is that your husband in the photo?" It was four years ago when Laurent arranged a romantic trip to Venice for their anniversary. They were happy. Marie had asked a tourist to take their picture in the Piazza San Marco. At the last minute the ice cream Laurent was holding fell right down the front of his shirt, making his wife and all the witnesses in the background laugh. Marie thinks about the dinner this evening. She doesn't know how she's going to hide everything from start to finish without arousing suspicion.

She's having lunch with Hervé today. He tells her how helpless he feels with his wife and daughter. Yesterday they had the nerve to open the cage that housed a turtledove he found six years ago in the woods in Orne. When he came home at the end of his day's work he found the cage empty but for a few feathers, and his wife and daughter laughed in his face at his despair. Marie finds this unbearably sad and wonders just how much pain you can cause another person without suffering any physical consequences. The two women are being so cruel, surely Hervé's distress will eventually spill over into violence. A good gunshot in the head to each.

Laurent comes home earlier than usual so he has time to get ready for dinner. Marie is rummaging frantically through her walk-in closet, she has no idea which dress to wear for dinner. Too dark an outfit would only emphasize her mood. Something too colorful might be misinterpreted as a sign of happiness. Pants are out of the question, her vulva can't tolerate the pressure of thick fabric. She can't wear panties, just very fine pantyhose. Laurent notices this when she takes off a dress for the tenth time. He comes over to her from behind, strokes her breasts, and plants a kiss in the crook of her neck. "You're very sexy in your pantyhose...We could get to work already, you know...We still have a little time." She's forgotten about the baby. The plan that so thrilled her only two days ago now seems laughable, stupid, disgusting.

Laurent is turned on, she can feel him hardening against her buttocks. She lets him have his way, can't see any alternative. She's never rejected him, he'd think it was odd if she did now for no obvious reason. Being

tired won't always be an excuse for escaping her conjugal duty, especially if they're still planning to have
a baby. Laurent lowers her pantyhose, turns his wife
around in his arms and lays her down on the bed. His
hand slips inside her, strokes her with slow circular
movements. He kisses her, explores her mouth with his
tongue, takes a handful of her hair, pinches her nipples
between thumb and forefinger. Marie is frightened it
will hurt. She prepares for the pain she will feel when
he penetrates her, taking a breath in and letting it out
slowly. He drives into her. Her body tears on the inside
as if a great heated file were being inserted into her vagina. Her mouth twists and she groans in pain. Laurent
pushes harder. Every thrust of his hips, the least undu-
lation is torture. She suddenly feels as if she is being
drained of all her blood, she can feel her organs sliding
downward inside her, a gaping wound opening up in her
stomach. Laurent plunges a finger into her anus and she
screams. He pulls it out. She feels raped all over again,
by her husband. He's not noticing her, is tormenting her
body, inflicting superficial pain to escape the confines
of an excitement that's become all too familiar. Now
there's no distinguishing between the two situations.
Her rapist's sadism feels to her just like Laurent's, the
husband who doesn't notice her suffering. "I'm coming…Wait, I'm coming…" He comes inside her. She's
going to throw up, represses it. A few vestiges of her

lunch come into her mouth. She smiles at him, puts her arms around him, breaks away. He watches in silence as she gets up. He can't possibly know that this second ordeal endured by his wife marks the end of any compromising on her part.

．
．
．

This dinner is a bad idea. On the way there Marie thinks about how she's going to say hello to her friends, about the moment when she has to sit down at the table, evading certain questions, certain forms of eye contact. Paul and his wife Sophia live in the Monge neighborhood. Marie and Laurent had hesitated for a long time before settling on their apartment in Charonne; they'd been offered an exceptional property on the rue Daubenton but didn't yet have the funds to afford it, much to the disappointment of Marie and Sophia, who'd been friends for years and liked to go to the Sunday market together on the rue Mouffetard.

"Are you staying in the car, or what?" Agreeing to make love with Laurent before the meal was also a bad idea. Her body had begged her to stop but it was too late and now she must simply wait for the pain to subside a little. Marie finds it hard to get out of the car. Her husband slams the door, doesn't notice the trouble she's having. "I do like Charonne but you gotta admit this neighborhood's quieter. It's better for kids." He still hasn't given up.

Paul and Sophia have a three-year-old son and live in a large duplex apartment. He's a gynecologist and she a dental surgeon. Marie has always found it practical having friends with a medical bent, but this evening she's wary of Paul's experience. After the rape she thought of the sexual diseases she might pass on to Laurent and the psychological trauma of abused women, but she hopes she can forget, erase all the suffering of this period. She's going to take refuge in her work and her marriage. Perhaps the longing to have a child with her husband will resurface in a few days, stronger than before.

Sophia appears on the landing looking radiant in a loose-fitting orange tunic. She takes Marie warmly in her arms. A delicious smell of Middle Eastern spices hangs in the air in their living room. "I made a couscous—Granny Zara's recipe!" Sophia was born in Morocco. She's proud of her roots and makes a point of passing on a few words of Arabic to her son so that he's familiar with his second culture. Paul is not very enthusiastic about this and thinks it will end up giving the child identity issues. "There she goes again! We're not in the medina now, baby!" They tease each other, laugh about it, understand each other. Marie envies their natural intimacy. Maybe Paul would have known straightaway, unlike Laurent.

Every subject they broach around the table strikes her as dull. She's distracted, far removed from the dinner, aware of the sounds without really hearing or understanding them. She stares blankly in one direction and then turns and alights on another. A few words ring out: "She was covered in bruises. Her body swollen and bleeding. She was most likely raped several times." Marie's eyes light up, her body is electrified, she wakes up at last. Paul is talking about one of his patients, a girl of seventeen who was beaten by her father for years and probably raped by him, and who came to see Paul in his office after a violent altercation. "When I examined her everything was confirmed. I didn't even need a speculum." There's a brief silence. The subject is disturbing, a bit disgusting. Sophia gets up to fetch the couscous from the kitchen while Paul continues to give details of the story.

Laurent doesn't seem put out, continues to chew absentmindedly on his piece of bread, as if to pass the time. "But are you sure it's the father? No, it's just these days it seems like everyone's been raped and the perpetrators are named before anyone can be sure it's really them." Marie doesn't say anything, this contribution smacks her full in the face. She feels dirty and ashamed before her husband, suddenly guilty for what she may have provoked the night before. Paul is used to this sort of discussion and tries to present a different argument. Good, evil, men accused of rape turning out to be victims of spite, the public lynching of some men, the Dominique Strauss-Kahn case, Polanski...

Sophia comes back into the dining room and puts a large colorful earthenware dish on the table. The couscous is almost overflowing. "Maybe we could talk about something else? I mean we could do without your work stories about rape when we're trying to eat." Marie wants them to talk about it. She wants to get up and scream that she too has been raped, by her boss, and she understands this young girl. She wants to announce loud and clear to her husband and friends that she was forced to take a penis in her mouth, in her ass and in her vagina, that her body was butchered, she had blood on her thighs, semen in the corner of her mouth, puke all over her breasts, and shit spread over her stomach. She could do it. Her mind fights to speak out. But she doesn't have the courage. She's afraid she'll destroy everything, lose her husband and friends, be judged, be suspected of lying or exaggerating. She decides against it.

They move on to something else. The subject is changed. "So, Laurent told us the good news. Enjoy yourselves while you can because they don't leave you in peace for a single night in the first year!" The baby again. Marie doesn't think she can keep this up. Her vagina feels stretched, torn between her thighs. She slips away to the bathroom, as natural as can be. Her breathing accelerates, on the verge of a panic attack. The walls close in, the paintings hanging along the corridor talk to her, criticizing her weakness. Uncontrollable tears spill down her cheeks, distorting her face, smudging her makeup. Her reflection appears. She looks like a whore. A raped whore. A few smears of blood seep into the toilet paper.

When she joins the others again, there are North African gazelle horn pastries proudly displayed on the table. "Is everything okay? You look a little tired this evening." Marie smiles, claims she hasn't been feeling too good since yesterday. Her husband puts his arms around her, cuddles her, and says they'll leave soon. Marie drains her coffee as she listens to Sophia's ideas for their next winter vacation. The four of them could go to Switzerland together. Her mother will look after their son. Skiing in the glorious alpine landscapes around Geneva, nothing better just before Christmas.

Marie is mortified, she realizes just how much the future means to people. No one ever talks about the present, and not much about the past. The evening when she was raped is already long ago, almost forgotten, obsolete. Even if she spoke about it publicly, she couldn't be sure how people would react. She'll have to see her attacker in the workplace, maybe even accept his congratulations for the contract she will soon have signed, walking beside him, smiling at him and smelling his aftershave. He will have forgotten, time will pass, and justice will too. The facts will have lapsed.

It's time to go home. Paul hands Marie her coat and wants to help her put it on. She refuses his offer, not wanting him to touch her. She thinks about his penis, about how he might take Sophia. She pictures him examining his young patient, imagines her tortured, abused vagina, its flesh and nerves raw. Sophia hears her son crying and kisses Marie before hurrying upstairs to soothe him.

"I've always thought it odd for a man to be a gynecologist. Seriously, it's kind of weird looking at vaginas all day long, isn't it?" The walls of the arcades by the Louvre Museum are so old, rising out of the ground since forever, solid as rocks. She'd liked to turn the steering wheel, for Laurent to hurtle into them, for the two of them to die instantly together, for him to shut up at last. He puts his hand on his wife's thigh. She automatically pushes it away as if terrified. Everything seems so easy to him. "Are you sure you're okay? You were a little strange over dinner." Marie gives up, puts his hand back on her leg and slides it a little way toward her crotch. Laurent smiles again. She wants him to stroke her, she thrusts his hand inside her pantyhose and rubs his penis at the same time. He has an erection. It's late. There's very little traffic along the riverbank. The bright light of streetlamps intermittently illuminates the inside of the car. At night Paris is sparklingly beautiful. Laurent has taken a wrong turn. The Hôtel de Ville is deserted, its white stone illuminated by dazzling reflections from the Seine. His penis hardens as Marie rubs it backward and forward. Her hand accelerates. He sighs, moans, raises his foot from the accelerator. She makes him come in a few minutes. Her hand is sticky, cloying. She disguises her disgust, looks for a Kleenex in the glove compartment to wipe herself. "Oh, I think you have your period, honey." His fingers emerge from her pantyhose soaked in blood. She tells him it's nothing, just the remains of her last period. Actually, no, she was raped a day ago, her insides torn in places till they bled while he was enjoying a lobster at the Coupole brasserie with his client.

He won't try anything this evening. Marie can go to bed without worrying. She'll let the time sift through her fingers. She knows that sometimes it will be tough, insurmountable, but she's sure she can do it. A whole new day starts tomorrow. Laurent gets into bed, kisses her. He's asleep already.

Bois-le-Roi is a delightful place. The Forest of Fontainebleau protects its inhabitants, nestling them in a natural, leafy cradle of calm. The reddish facades of the large buhrstone buildings peep through the impressive oak trees that edge the old properties. Below them the Seine flows past. They can hear the sound of the water, the pressure of it. This is where they've chosen to have their picnic. In crisp beams of autumn sunlight Marie's mother, Irene, is busy unwrapping the picnic basket she prepared this morning. A multitude of bread rolls arranged perfectly by flavor give the finishing touch to the bucolic mood of the scene.

It's nearly three weeks since Marie's assault. Her vagina has stopped hurting. The pain inflicted by her rape has disappeared, taking with it the few precise recollections that clung to her memory. She has continued to make love with her husband. He still hasn't noticed anything unusual about her behavior, just a few bad moods put down to stress and tiredness.

Laurent is unfolding the fishing rods down by the river with his father-in-law, Gérard. They're hoping to grill their catch this evening. Marie's father, a retired pharmacist, has always exercised a kindly authority over his family. His wife, a stay-at-home mother who attentively raised their two daughters, showed no inclination to have a career. Being a mother was enough for her. Marie has never thought to ask her whether she was truly happy, whether having a child could fill the void that she sometimes feels opening up around her. "Children are life itself," her mother often tells her. "When life is added to life, what more could you want to give meaning to everything else?"

Marie is helping her sister change her baby's diaper on the plaid blanket. He seems to like his aunt. She forces a smile.

"How are things at the bank? I heard it was heating up right now." The pitiful ordinariness of the questions Marie has to answer shoots through her head at the speed of sound. Is she such a good actor? How can this loving, affectionate, attentive family, this husband who's so close to his wife, not see anything, how come not one of them has noticed the change in her? They're uncorking the champagne, handing around petit fours on china plates. It's absurdly cheerful. Marie feels like taking the big knife, snatching it from her mother and, in sheer desperation, driving it straight into her heart and slicing it down into her belly.

Laurent comes back, swinging the half-full bag of fish from one hand to the other. He's pleased. Marie finds him uglier by the minute. With his fishing rod, his blissful look of permanent happiness, and his perfect little life, she feels like spitting on him, ramming something right down his throat. Someone needs to focus on the details in this tableau that has no visible flaws. No one thinks to do that, preferring instead the smooth, supple contours of reassuring surface emotions. Whatever happens they wouldn't want to make out the black stains, the dysfunction and the torment. Marie remembers how shocked she was when she first saw Magritte's paintings on a trip to Brussels with Laurent. She'd always been fascinated by the precision of his work, the almost photographic mastery of his subject, his perfect grasp of the laws of perspective, but was terribly disappointed. Proximity can shatter everything in an instant. As she moved closer to her favorite work, *The Castle of the Pyrenees*, featuring a huge rock suspended in the sky with a small medieval town on its summit, she noticed the first imperfections. The irregular brushstrokes, the rough-hewn curves and contours, cracks in the paint...It was so disappointing, so far removed from everything she'd envisioned about this artistic perfection that she'd believed in since she first came across the painting as a child, on the glossy paper of a school book.

The sun illuminates the scene. Its gilded beams light up the damp lawn, radiate through the air. Only Marie is surrounded by gloom. In total darkness. She has the same faltering feeling as in that museum. The veil is finally being lifted on her existence, crushing the idealistic lie. She longs for silence to think over what she can do to extricate herself. They all clink their glasses. Marie feels like snapping the tablecloth out from under them as they guzzle champagne and maca-roons, she wants to topple them over like glasses, break the crockery and dump everything on the ground. She never wants to feel her vagina again. Neither the suf-fering nor the arousal that are destroying her day after day. No one will ever touch her again.

"What's this, then? Don't you like champagne any-more?" her father says. "And I thought it would make you happy, it's your favorite!" He puts his strong arms around her, squeezing her a little too tightly. Within a second she's driven away her thoughts and buried her longings and is smiling at him. She eats and drinks, and kisses her husband, mother, and sister. She forgets the details, camouflages the flaws, ejects the pain, represses her disgust at the indifference of her loved ones. Their lunch is over. They need to go home, Roxane's baby is getting cold.

Marie clings to her Monday morning delay like a precious undying feature. Some things mustn't change. Laurent found his file right away, he'll be on time. He wanted to make love to Marie last night. She couldn't refuse, she gave herself to him with complete abandon. She lost that game long ago. The memories are gradually being quashed in her mind. She puts her cup in the sink and suddenly feels dizzy. Then it stops. She's not sleeping well at the moment and, when Laurent's not looking, she takes a lot of sleeping tablets before bed. Maybe the pills' harmful side effects are making her weaker than usual.

She heads off to the bank on her new bicycle. Hervé's happy to see her and shows her a picture on his cell phone of the turtledove he decided to buy on Saturday at a pet store on the banks of the Seine. "The look on Corinne's face when she realized the cage had a new occupant! I just saw that and I knew I was going to have the best weekend of my life!"

Marie goes to her office for her nine-thirty meeting. She puts down her coffee and turns on her computer.

Her stomach clenches, her eyes glaze over. Time stands still, the taste of urine comes back to her. Her vagina contracts, instinctively protecting itself. Her old cell phone has been placed in the middle of her desk. Marie can still feel it vibrating at her feet in that car. She remembers the configuration of the screen, the colors, the rhythm of the new message ringtone, her finger typing away on the keypad a few minutes before the attack. He has been in this office. He's decided to come back into her life. She slowly picks up the cell phone. "Oh yes, the CEO's assistant came by this morning. He found your cell after the last meeting, he wanted to give it back to you in person but you'd left already." He's lying to everyone too. She's not the only one. She's strangely reassured by this thought, it brings her closer to him in the intimacy of their shared secret. They're in the same boat, perhaps even in the same dead end. When she's plugged the phone in to charge it she switches it on, rereads Laurent's messages, now finds them appallingly childish, thoughtless, almost indecent. Why did the CEO want to give her back her phone? There's no evidence left now. He's completely in the clear, it would be her word against his. No gynecological examination, no traces of violence, his car must have been cleaned from top to bottom the very next day, Marie threw her clothes into the dumpster. No one knows about it, it's too late, the moment has passed.

Her client arrives late and she asks for him to wait in the corridor. She feels like throwing up. She runs to the bathroom, flips up the lid, and spews out her breakfast. It's too much of a shock. Everything's getting more and more complicated. One thing leading to another. But life just keeps on doing the opposite of what she wants, and she decides that today must go ahead without a letup.

:

A section of boulevard Voltaire is blocked because of a strike. The warm croissants will go cold. "You need to take rue Richard-Lenoir," a policeman tells her, and she has an urge to retort that that was the street where she was raped and she doesn't feel like walking along it, and, as an agent of the law, he should find another solution by way of compensation. She doesn't say anything. The entrance to the car park isn't all that wide, after all. It was dark, but Marie suddenly thinks it strange that no one saw anything. She pictures people turning away at the point where the deepest core of her parted company with the rest of her body, people happier to stare straight ahead than witness that disturbing sex scene. She doesn't stop, quickens her step, gets away from the place by crossing the street. A furtive moment of suffering that stirs memories. She doesn't remember the pain now.

Laurent is only just waking. He went to bed late last night after finishing his defense. The trial starts soon. He gets up to kiss his wife. "How lucky am I to have such a wonderful wife... She brings croissants for breakfast. I didn't even hear you go out!" She didn't want to wake him and run the risk of being subjected to his morning sexual enthusiasm. She sets the table meticulously, arranges the five croissants on the large silver dish her parents gave them as a wedding present, and pours freshly squeezed orange juice into a jug. Laurent starts cooking eggs and bacon, filling the room with the smell of frying. "Can you open the window a little, otherwise the whole living room smells of it." She gets up. Her stomach churns again. How many times has she thrown up in the last few days?

Laurent looks at her. "Hey, are you okay? Are you sick?" She hurries to the bathroom and doesn't have time to close the door. Laurent watches her through the half-open doorway and smiles.

"What are you laughing at? Watching me on all fours, puking?" Laurent comes over to her but she pushes him away. She finds the situation disgusting and asks him to go back to the kitchen and finish making breakfast. It hurts deep down in her stomach. She can't take any more of this aching. It's always in the same place, as if the pain has made up its mind to keep knocking at the same door, reopening the wound with the same determination. Marie has nothing left to throw up, she's spitting bile. The green liquid dribbles down the inside of the toilet bowl. She drags herself back to join Laurent. He's sitting on a chair, slightly offended that she banished him so harshly. He gets the picture before she does.

Marie sits at the table without a word, still wincing because of the acid that keeps rising up her throat. She can feel Laurent staring at her. She looks him right in the eye until he gives up and looks away. She doesn't want to know what he's thinking, doesn't want to hear the words come out of his mouth. If she listens to his explanations she'll scream, spit in his face, try to push him out the window at any opportunity or chuck the hot oil from the bacon in his face. "I'd rather stay at home today, I'm a little tired from the week I've had." He was planning to go to an exhibition at the Musée d'Orsay, which Marie loves visiting on Saturday mornings before tourists get all overexcited about Paris. The light there soothes her; soft vaporous beams filter through the glass roof of this former train station, casting a heavenly protective halo over the large marble statues. He won't go alone, he'll get on with his work or go visit his parents in Melun.

Marie returns to the bedroom to get some rest, burrowing back under the unmade sheets contentedly. Some days aren't worth the effort of being lived anywhere but in bed. She can just see herself in her pajamas, slumped on her plump comfortable mattress, receiving clients, friends, and relations. The nausea is back, stronger than before. "Do we have any medicine for this? Something to stop me throwing up?" Laurent brings a pack of small red pills and a glass of water. She'd like to tear the smile off his face, peel off his skin, blot out any trace of satisfaction in him. He needs to leave, and plants a kiss on his wife's forehead like an encouragement for what lies ahead. She's going to sleep all day. Sleep at last. For a few hours she just won't be here.

Marie has never been particularly fond of her mother-in-law, Jeanne. She finds her too invasive, protecting Laurent like a persecuted little boy, studying every move he makes so she can then give her advice on absolutely everything. Marie hates unplanned visits, and even more so now. "She insisted, I really couldn't turn her away!" Marie wanted to make the most of this week of vacation to get some rest, staying in bed to read and eat chocolate. Laurent is showering his increasingly fragile wife with thoughtful attention. Jeanne arrives at lunchtime with a large apple tart. Marie reflects that the woman must have spent more time in her life baking than taking care of herself. But she can't see any similarities between Jeanne and her own mother, even though the rather broad status of homemaker—taking care of the house, cooking, raising children, and ensuring her husband's happiness—is virtually identical for the two women. There are just different levels of submissiveness. Marie's mother is less ridiculous in her duties than Jeanne. That's just an aspect of personality, though, because her mother cultivates a more obvious elegance and restraint. Where would Marie be on this scale? At what point would she be capable of going against everything her environment has taught her?

"Oh my, sweetheart, you looked tired! We should go out to get some air after lunch, go have some tea in the Luxembourg Gardens." Jeanne's perfume, an unrelenting combination of incense, sandalwood, and musk that Marie often recognizes in the street on older women, reawakens her nausea. She endures the meal with the same revulsion that she harbors for vaudeville: it's too loud, the stage is overcrowded, and the laughter is exaggerated. She needs a pause in this torment so she slips away to the bathroom. The walls aren't very thick and she hears her mother-in-law mutter something to Laurent. She can't make out the words, almost certainly some criticism about the frozen quiche she's served.

When Marie returns there's silence in the room. "I'm not really feeling up to going for a walk today, but you go without me." Jeanne eyes her tenderly, looking her up and down, lingering over her figure and virtually undressing her. Laurent purses his lips and nods his head approvingly. Marie finishes her slice of apple tart in silence. Sugary snacks are the only thing she can keep down at the moment. Jeanne and Laurent decide they will go out.

"In case you have a problem, honey, I'll have my cell. You just call and I'll be here." She thinks this comment stupid. She'd like to ask him where he was when she was being raped. Now he wants her reassurance over a simple stomach bug. What a farce. She gives Jeanne a peck on the cheek, keeping away from her like someone with the flu, then apologizes about the quiche and heads back to bed.

Sunday is Marie's favorite day in Paris. It's the day she and Sophia go to the big market on the rue Mouffetard in the Fifth Arrondissement. She likes strolling around that street for hours. She knows all the traders and they know she's a loyal customer. The small bakery stall is between displays of cheeses and fish. When it's the season this is where she comes to buy her game, and then she makes a big steaming casserole of wild boar or venison stew for the whole family.

She's trying to put on her dress to go meet Sophia on the place Monge, but is having trouble doing it up. Laurent comes into the room and offers to help. "That's strange, it must have shrunk in the wash. Or I've been eating too much at my mom's house the last few days." Laurent doesn't say anything, he doesn't want to rush his wife with his inane happiness. She never wears much makeup, just foundation and lipstick. Despite her efforts, her greasy skin doesn't give her much option. Tiny red patches like insect bites are proliferating over her face. She looks terrible. Dark rings run along the curve of her eyes, deepening the green of her irises. Her brown hair, which she washed only yesterday, is lank. She's distressed by her reflection. As she has done every time she's been out this week, she puts a pantyliner in her underwear. She'll be getting her period, it's just a little late. She loathes the wet trickling feeling and not being prepared. Laurent comes into the room to say goodbye to her and kisses her neck. She turns away slightly, can no longer bear to be touched. The attentive gestures of those close to her are becoming a source of sadness and suffering worse than a disease. She feels as if she shouldn't go out, but the sun is shining after endless rainy days, the bells of Saint-Médard's church will ring at lunchtime, filling the streets of the old neighborhood with sweet nostalgia. Paris is holding its breath.

She'll feel unstoppable, carried along by the city she loves, reassured and grounded by the cobblestones on the rue Mouffetard.

When she arrives home Marie puts the dozen or so small bags down on the kitchen counter. She's bought too much cheese but she couldn't resist it. As she turns around she notices a pink-and-white box in the middle of the dining room table. She goes over to it. "My darling, to think you still don't get it...I love you so much." Laurent appears, startling her. She grabs hold of the box—it's a pregnancy test. Her hands are shaking, the pressure in her temples hammers behind her brows and feels as if it's pushing her forehead out of shape. A cold sweat bathes her stomach and neck.

"I'm not pregnant, I'm about to get my period." A week now Marie's been waiting for her body to bleed. She's always a few days late so she hasn't fretted. She can feel the disaster drawing closer, the lead wall she's going to crash into looming. Challenging her.

"Use it, then, if you're so sure of yourself. I know what I'm saying, you're my wife and I know your body. I'll wait out here."

Marie fulminates with anger. How dare he say he knows her body? This man who chose to penetrate her the very day after her rape, delving his great fat fingers deep into her injured vagina and lowering his head toward her crotch while he grabbed her by the hair. She doesn't want to take this test. Can't do it. If she does she'll go crazy. In this liberal society that rewards those who put in enough effort, she should be queen. Raped, soiled, humiliated, abandoned in her own shit, bathed in her attacker's still-warm semen, she could have put her trust in justice. She chose silence. Her husband's devastatingly knowing looks aggravate her nausea day by day. Laurent laughs, talks, goes out, drinks, cooks, and sleeps. Incapable of arousing even the tiniest whiff of pleasure in her when lovemaking. Marie thinks she might have a horrible feeling of dishonor if she tells Laurent the truth, but she tries desperately to convince herself that this would be only a small sacrifice in exchange for her freedom. In the end, though, she always resigns herself to the lies, aware she's betraying herself, destroying herself. Is it abandonment that she so dreads, giving up the emotional and material comfort that she's grown so attached to over the years, the whole sequence of past happiness and mutual love, or the reckless unhealthy adrenaline produced by secrecy? Maybe it's for all these reasons at the same time that she now can't refuse to take the test. She doesn't shy away from it.

Marie makes her way along the corridor toward the bathroom. She wants to turn back but she can't.

Laurent watches her from a distance, starts to follow her. She locks the door and opens the box to read the instructions. It's not very complicated, she just has to pee on the stick and wait for some lines to appear.

"Okay? Did you do it? Open up, I want to be with you to see the result." Under this much pressure, Marie could drown herself in the bathtub or slash her wrists with a razor. She has the choice of knowing how this will all end. Her breathing quickens, her heartbeats explode inside her chest, her ice-cold legs wobble on either side of the toilet bowl. She puts the cap on the test and stows it back inside the box. Laurent hammers frantically on the door. She eventually opens up and hands him the box. He takes it, grabbing it from her with an enthusiasm she's never seen in him before.

One line. She's not pregnant, she knew it. Laurent's disappointed. They can throw the test in the trash, move on to something else. The baby can happen another time. She heads back toward the kitchen but Laurent catches her by the arm. "Wait, wait, it's not over. Look!" A second, fainter line is appearing alongside the first. That's impossible, it was negative just a second ago. Very slowly, cruelly, the momentous second line gradually asserts itself until it's completely visible, establishing a definitive verdict. Two lines. Pregnant. Laurent explodes with happiness in his wife's arms. Marie doesn't know what to think. There has been road work on their street for months. She can hear the pneumatic drill breaking up concrete. They're pouring cement on her head. The heavy gravelly flow of it crushes down on her, immobilizes her, burns her, buries her. She's suffocating. She smiles at Laurent, bursts into tears, doubles up in pain, throws up, then smiles again, laughs out loud, cries. It's quite a performance. She already knows she can't take this. Marie is in no doubt at all: it isn't her husband's baby.

"I have to call my mother! She told me over lunch. I knew it, I can't tell you how happy I am. Our baby! Call your sister!"

She nods, hiding her distress. This pregnancy is a disgrace, it goes against nature. Until now, even after her rape, Marie has never really felt evil at work around her. Now there's a black shadow evolving in her womb, propagating through the nerves of her genitals, infesting her guts with its appalling stench. She collapses on the floor. Laurent's yelling into his phone in the living room. The chill of the floor tiles stiffens her body where it lies. Her first words are addressed to herself. "Your child will be cursed."

．
．
．

I don't know how but I knew it. I knew it would happen this year, I told your father!" Marie's mother can't hide her emotion. The whole family has been invited to lunch. Only her sister's husband, who's on a business trip to London, couldn't be here to celebrate the new pregnancy. Marie still smiles constantly, wanly brushing aside the multicolored sequins that Laurent has scattered over the tablecloth by way of decoration. It's diabolical. She wonders how she ended up here. This huge joke that everyone believes in, this stupid performance lighting up the faces of her beloved family as she looks at them with her guilty eyes.

Her father uncorks the second bottle of champagne. "To my baby, who's now going to have a baby of her own! I want to tell you just how proud your mother and I are of you, of who you are and everything that you and Laurent are about to start building together. We love you and we'll always be here. Well—you get to do the sleepless nights on your own!" Laughter erupts around the room; long blades slice through the air, sharks carving through water. The excess of happiness is intolerable.

Marie's mother keeps weeping in her daughter's arms and starts describing her experiences of motherhood. Marie doesn't want to hear this, would like to slap her to get her to shut up. She calls for a bit of quiet, a moment of calm. No one's listening. It's hopeless. Marie must open her presents. That's the least she deserves for carrying her rapist's child. Baby clothes, two maternity dresses, some crockery, little fleecy blankets, a stroller, and some toys. She still can't quite get her head around it. She's pregnant. As the weeks go by, it'll become really visible. Her stomach will grow, her body will change, and her breasts will fill with milk that she hopes will be so bitter that her baby can't suckle.

Roxane has a very special gift for her. Marie tears the wrapping paper off the heavy package that looks at first glance like a book. On the cover Roxane herself has put together a mixture of whimsical stickers and a collage of photos from Marie's childhood. Marie could almost collapse with pain. Roxane thinks that she's moved to tears and stands behind her, turning the pages for her. A newborn Marie in her mother's arms at the hospital. Marie aged six riding a pony. Marie skiing with her father, who's teaching her to snowplow. Marie at her first teenage party at high school. Marie receiving her diploma at business school. Marie at the *mairie* in Bois-le-Roi formalizing her union with Laurent. Marie in a swimsuit on her honeymoon in Bali. Marie getting ready for her first day at the bank.

She gives up. She's going to tell them now, this can't go on. Where's the picture of her rape? Where should they put this latest memory, the only one that can end it all, taint it all, spill its bile over this whole catalogue of perfection? The ideal woman no longer exists. There's no woman now, no wife, no sister, and no daughter. There's just the filth, anger, and darkness in her crotch sitting there right in front of them all. These memories are now all fake. Everything's ruined. "All that's missing now is the baby." The baby she won't allow to live. She can't. Can she bear to have the eyes of her rapist's progeny on her every day? The cruelty of watching Laurent get a bottle ready every morning for a child she knows isn't his? That monster is inside her womb.

Roxane closes the photo album and puts her arms around her sister. Her little boy is crying in his high chair but Marie pretends not to hear her nephew's wails. "Come on, you need to get some practice!" Roxane says, picking up her son and putting him carefully into her sister's arms. An indescribable pain cuts across the small of her back. Marie feels as if she's going to fall apart any minute, breaking up under the pressure here at the foot of the sofa. The child squirms furiously, kicking his cold little feet against Marie's breasts. He swivels his eyes in every direction, twists his huge head from right to left, unable to settle. He screams, aware that something's not right. Laurent comes over to help Marie and she hands the baby to him, relieved and a little ashamed. A subtle embarrassment creeps over the family. Roxane smiles and looks away. Her mother averts her eyes. Laurent is a father already, taking the child as if he were his own, petting him, wrapping him up in love and affection, smothering him with attention.

It's three o'clock already and someone says, "Let's leave the mom-to-be to get some rest!" The words slap at Marie's ears like the ring of an alarm clock that no one's thought to turn off on vacation. She was just chatting to her father about contracts at work, about her most important client who's about to sign a million-euro life insurance policy, and about her plans for a career in a private bank. It was an interesting subject. For a few minutes she'd almost forgotten. The baby has ruined everything all over again. She knows that soon, with her disgusting big belly, it will be impossible to forget her torment for a second. That won't happen. She'll have a secret abortion. It'll just take a bit of organization and discretion. The evening she found out she was pregnant Marie tried to find a solution on the Internet, typing "pregnancy after rape" into the search engine. It didn't take that much to summarize the situation, just those three words, but it was the first time she succeeded in putting that night into precise terms. France is a tolerant, society-focused country. The Veil law has allowed voluntary terminations since 1975. Before twelve weeks' gestation any woman can choose to have an abortion, whatever her reasons. Marie will find a doctor and explain the situation. She'll be protected by medical confidentiality, no one will know. She'll take the last pill, the one that triggers the evacuation of the fetus, before going to bed in the evening. She's prepared to suffer alone and in silence for a few hours, and it will all be over in the morning. A miscarriage. It often happens in the early months. The blood-soaked sheets will be reliable evidence of the tragedy. Laurent will be devastated for a few days. They'll make love again and this time she'll be pregnant with his child.

Not many people are brave enough to cycle in winter. Laurent wants his wife to protect herself from the cold, gently scolding her to be sure she avoids any risks, tying her scarf around her neck before she leaves for work. Black ice, Parisian drivers in the morning rush— he's worried for her. Marie spends her time reassuring him, even though she wants the worst to happen: being knocked over by a truck or skidding under a car would be the best thing that could happen to her. Her womb empty at last.

"I'll come pick you up from work in the car this evening. Paul's expecting us in his office at seven. I can't wait! The first ultrasound, maybe we'll get to see something..." She thinks he's pathetic. He kisses her and goes off to work, forgetting his file which is over by the window. Marie sees it but doesn't say anything, starting to take pleasure in his misfortune. Laurent has insisted that Paul oversee her pregnancy from start to finish. Which is an additional disaster for Marie. It will make everything more difficult to implement, he'll notice every attempt she makes, and she won't be able to confide in him like a normal patient. He's married to her best friend, and she can't even tell *her* the truth. The escape route is getting narrower.

On the way to the bank her cell vibrates: Laurent wants to know if she arrived safely. She won't reply for thirty minutes, time enough for him to fret. Her phone's never rung so much: Sophia calls to say she'll be there this evening for her first appointment with

Paul; her sister wants to have lunch with her tomorrow; her mother's going to make a hearty stew for their visit on Sunday; Laurent's worried because she didn't eat enough breakfast. It never stops.

Hervé is in deeper despair than usual this morning—his wife tried to poison the turtledove last night. He saw the open pack of rat poison under the kitchen sink. Marie has her doubts about his wife's true intentions...Maybe she's planning to kill him, not the bird? But she keeps this to herself, doesn't want to tell him. The day wears on. Her work has now become a pastime, a hobby that keeps her tortured mind occupied while she waits to see what happens next in the tragic saga.

It's six thirty when Laurent calls to say he's waiting outside in the car. Marie hurries out. He's badly parked, right in the middle of the street with his lights flashing amid a cacophony of car horns and insults. Laurent yells out the window for her to hurry up. In her rush, she knocks into a buggy and the baby howls. "Oh my God, what the hell! You need to look where you're going, you could have killed him!" Those last words resonate in her. She feels like snatching up the child, taking him from his mother, and hurling him to the ground until his brain spills from his skull. Striking him again and again, hard enough to bury him in the concrete. She apologizes and runs on to the car. Still shocked, she doesn't kiss her husband but just asks him to pull away quickly.

"Here she is, the mom-to-be! My darling!" Sophia always overdoes things. She literally throws herself at Marie, kissing her ostentatiously, hugging her face up to hers and pressing against her body. Marie realizes she doesn't like tactile people. The sort who innocently touch a hand, a shoulder, or a thigh as if they don't know they're doing it. The smell of disinfectant hanging in the air in the corridor turns her stomach. Paul's office is in the obstetrics and gynecology department in a wing of the Salpêtrière hospital. Paul is a little older than Laurent, and they met thanks to Sophia and Marie's long-standing friendship. It was friendship at first sight for the two men, true friends, always there for each other. Marie remembers when Paul and Sophia's baby was born: she and Laurent arrived in the maternity ward laden with presents and boxes of chocolates, running along the corridors so as not to be the last to see the baby. Now it's their turn. Marie imagines the worst, plagued by irrational anxieties: What if the ultrasound reveals the rape? What if the fetus doesn't have Laurent's face, isn't the same shape as him, doesn't move or smile like him? What if Paul finds evidence of the rape when he examines her? She thinks that such a highly reputed gynecologist who's used to seeing rape victims sometimes several days after the assault couldn't miss what happened to her. A woman's body talks, bears witness to the violence it has suffered. She suddenly regrets her irresponsibility—Paul is going to know everything in the first few seconds, he'll look up and ask everyone to leave the room so he can ask her for some explanations.

"Come on then, you, onto the chair! Let's see if Dad did a good job. If it's a boy I hope he won't inherit his father's physique!" They all burst out laughing. The atmosphere is relaxed, lighthearted. Marie hovers in the middle of it all. Surrounded and alone, supported and abandoned by everyone. Maybe this is the right time for them to find out the truth, after all? Marie undresses behind the small screen. She comes out, coyly, takes a few hesitant steps toward Paul, tugging the bottom of her sweater down over the tops of her thighs. Laurent is touched by his wife's shyness. Marie settles herself on the examination chair, her legs shaking in the stirrups.

"I'm going to do the scan. Don't worry, it doesn't hurt."

She feels like an animal, a fat heifer having her parts examined while three prurient strangers look on. Paul inserts the speculum, the cold implement slides between, presses against, and then painfully widens the walls of her vagina before easing out slowly. She holds her breath for a moment. Paul looks rattled. His face freezes. She can tell the revelation is about to happen, is almost relieved that the truth is finally going to explode in everyone's face and this masquerade can come to an end.

The scan begins. Paul picks up a long, round-ended plastic tube covered in slimy gel, and introduces it progressively into her while glancing at the screen set up facing him. He types on his keyboard, concentrating and serious. All at once a wide smile relaxes the muscles of his face.

"Look, there it is. The fetus is very small at the moment, but you'll be able to see something in a few weeks." Marie doesn't want to look. Paul thinks she hasn't noticed the screen intended for patients that's hanging on the right-hand wall. He points it out, almost prepared to turn her head toward it. "Here, look. Take a look, it's there." She can make out a large white halo in the middle of which Paul points out what looks like a little black clot. Laurent comes over to his wife's side. He's crying. Paul comforts him with a bevy of solid masculine slaps on the shoulder. Marie looks away from the screen. The fetus doesn't yet have any human characteristics: no head, no feet, and no genitals. But soon it will all appear, it will materialize. There'll be appointments like this every month.

Marie gets up awkwardly from the chair to go and get dressed. From behind the screen she can hear Sophia's exuberant cries: "The champagne's on me this evening! The first scan!" Another party celebrating the rape. Marie doesn't remember being this enthusiastic when her nephew or Sophia's baby was born. It's as if everyone knows about her assault and wants to make her pay for lying by going over the top with delight about her pregnancy; a simple case of revenge.

"You do have a little yeast infection that needs treating. Apart from that, everything's perfectly normal. We'll have a checkup every month or two." A yeast infection. The dumb explanation for Paul's frowning. He prints out an image of the scan as a memento. Laurent wants to frame it. Meanwhile, the real evidence has completely disappeared, the file has been closed with no repercussions. The only thing left to console Marie is the child of that abuse.

"To new life! To my best friend's baby! To the woman you've grown into, whom I've loved and admired day after day for fifteen years!" They all raise their glasses. Marie smiles, a glass of Coca-Cola in her hand. She thinks that if Sophia knew the truth, she surely wouldn't admire her as much. Laurent kisses his wife. The other customers in the Rotonde restaurant congratulate the young woman from a distance. Next week Laurent and Marie will start work in their apartment getting the baby's nursery ready. Their old study will no longer exist, they need to make room for the child. Marie will have to sacrifice her own space, as well as her time and her body, to ensure the preparations for the new arrival are perfect. It's a little like organizing a surprise birthday party for her boss. The restaurant is sumptuously decorated. Marie's favorite thing in Paris is the old brasseries with their Belle Époque atmosphere, the elegance of their agile staff gliding between the tables with their Parisian accents and grouchy temperaments, the simple but delicious French fare always served on plates stamped with the brasserie's name. All those places she loved to visit before her rape now make her wish she were dead. She's stopped listening to the conversation, is vaguely aware that they're discussing the wallpaper for the baby's room.

"The duck breast with porcini mushrooms and pureed potatoes for madame." Laurent asks if he can taste it. She hates people wanting to taste other people's food, wanting to swap mouthfuls to see the difference and ending up with food envy.

"With my first it was as easy as posting a letter. My husband had a tougher time than I did," a tall overdressed woman at the next table contributes to the conversation. Everyone offers their opinion or comments on their own experience. No one notices her silence. The curtain goes up and they each play their part in this absurd performance. Laurent is drunk, hooting with pride that he'll soon be a father and laying his hand on his wife's stomach. People smile sentimentally at his happiness—it's only natural.

When the meal is over Paul pays the bill and Sophia helps Marie up, lifting her with extreme care as if she's now paraplegic. The boulevard du Montparnasse is still busy, cars hurtling along the wide, brightly lit street. They decide to take a taxi home. There's a truck that will be abreast of them in just a few seconds, bowling along quickly. It could kill Marie, crush her outright. She need only take three steps and throw herself in its path to end her torment right now. She moves forward, breaks away. Her leading foot steps off the sidewalk. She's pulled back by the arm. "What are you doing, honey? The taxi stand on this side. You're tired, let's get you home." Marie is lost, isolated.

As they reach the taxi stand, she makes eye contact with an elderly lady crossing the street to go into the restaurant. She suddenly feels understood. This woman has the same look in her eye as she does, she's been raped too, Marie's sure of it. It's a mutual understanding, a connection between two women who recognize each other. Marie breaks away from Laurent to go speak to her, claiming that the woman is a good client of hers. Laurent is taken aback but waits next to the taxi and chats with Paul and Sophia, still watching his wife. She runs to catch up with the woman and takes hold of her hand. Marie's desperate eyes look directly at her. "You know, I can see it, you know what's wrong with me, what happened to me." The woman looks at her for a moment, then her face changes. She doesn't understand, asks her whether they know each other, if she has some problem that needs her help. Marie instantly lets go of her hand. It was a mistake. She's got the wrong person, a silly mistake, an impression. She apologizes, mortified by her madness which is now out in the open right in front of her.

She heads back along the boulevard to join Laurent. "So, everything okay? I didn't know you talked to clients outside of the office." They climb into the taxi. She was sure there had been a connection. She might never have an opportunity like that again in her life. Laurent watches his wife, the cognac on his breath filling the back of the car with its reek. Marie watches passersby through the window. Who would understand her nightmare? Who'll be there to help her, to get her out of this dead end? The answer suddenly stabs at her stomach. It's all so clear: she's on her own. She'll be alone from start to finish, she'll battle relentlessly against her child unaided. If she is to take action, the only thing she can rely on is her own instinct. The long-awaited anger she's been anticipating finally takes hold of her. Her husband has fallen asleep, his face crushed against the window. The taxi driver is silent. Over the lilting notes of an oriental melody, the softest whispering can be heard: "I don't have a choice. I don't have a choice. I don't have a choice…"

．
．
．

Marie's mother always greets them on the front steps to the house, her hands clasped together, a soft maternal glow in her eye, and her pleasure at spending the day as a family written all over her face. Roxane and her husband will be here soon. It's the fifth month and Marie's stomach has grown distinctly rounded. Laurent gets out of the car to help his wife out. She's wearing the maternity dress that her sister gave her; her own clothes stopped fitting her a couple of weeks ago now. "Here's the beauty! You look radiant." Obviously, that's not true. Marie has already put on a lot of weight. She spends her days slumped at her desk, gorging on potato chips and candy. When she arrives home in the evening she likes to make herself big Nutella sandwiches, potato-and-gherkin salads, or olive bread that she finishes single-handed, slouching on the sofa in all her lard. Laurent isn't concerned about her rampant appetite and thinks it natural for a pregnant woman to eat more than usual. Paul has concurred. Marie and Laurent go to his office every last Friday of the month—she never goes alone, and this lack of privacy means she hasn't been able to speak to Paul or give him the tiniest indication of her desperate situation. She's utterly cornered.

It's a very large, three-story house. Roxane has come into the living room with her husband, who's giving the baby his bottle. He warmly congratulates Marie and puts an arm around her. Julien is a good family man, a kind, loving, intelligent, attentive, sociable, and cultivated husband with an interesting job as a project manager for a firm of architects. He's one of those men with no visible faults, with no problem that might throw things off balance. One of the builders, the beavers, who, day after day, lay down the foundations, the bases for the infrastructure of their own lives. Marie was like that too before. Now she wishes she could bring it all crashing down with one swipe of her hand.

They move through to sit at the table. Marie's mother has made scallops in cream, one of Laurent's favorites. "We saw you on TV last night," she says as she brings the large steaming dish to the table. "Your husband's a star! Maybe your baby will be a lawyer too." A report on the Lancarde case was broadcast on one of the public channels the night before. Laurent gave an interview to the journalist running the investigation. He's embarrassed but happy to have something of an impact on Marie's family. "How about you, my darling?" she asks, turning to Marie. "Are you managing at work? Laurent said you were sick last week. Are you feeling better?"

Last week was the quarterly meeting, run once again by the area CEO, her rapist. When a colleague reminded Marie about the meeting the day before, she hesitated. She'd been thinking about it for a long time, had spent whole nights imagining different scenarios for this encounter. Should she face up to her attacker or avoid him? She chose the second option. There could have been three hundred people in the meeting room, Marie would still have felt the irrational fear of being raped by that man in front of all of them. She hasn't yet officially informed the bank's directors about her maternity leave. It's likely that her CEO is completely unaware that she's pregnant. And how will he react when he does find out? She has no way of knowing, she'll have to keep waiting.

For dessert they move through to the conservatory, harshly illuminated by the bright white light of the day. Marie devours the chocolate mousse her mother has made. She's not allowed any champagne, just a small glass of sweet cider. She has a peculiar respect for Paul's instructions: not to drink any alcohol, do a few exercises in the morning, sleep at regular hours, drink a lot of water, attend to her body with little massages. A real sort of therapy, an unnamable hypocrisy. She doesn't want anything to do with this baby—not the nausea, the permanent tiredness, the diarrhea, the acid reflux, the cellulite massacring her once smooth, firm body, the hot flashes of stinking sweat that soak her bedsheets, the greasy skin constantly dotted with red patches, the lank hair, or the dog's breath. The suffering's pointless, it's the sort experienced by pregnant women in the early days before they have an abortion. Their bodies are already changing, but their minds stay the same. They experience no happiness as the child grows inside them, they know it will never live.

Marie forgot to check her blood pressure this morning. Paul has asked her to check it every two weeks just as a precaution, after it dipped slightly last week. She has to go up to the second floor to fetch the monitor. "No, I'll get it darling," Laurent says. "You stay there." Marie snaps at him. She's not a child, she's had enough of being treated like an invalid. Laurent backs down but asks her to take good deep breaths as she goes up the stairs.

Being nostalgic by nature, Marie's mother chose not to touch her daughters' bedrooms after they left home. Every single thing has stayed in its allocated place, like a museum of memories; a large poster of horses, yellowing here and there, is still Scotch-taped above her bed, and there are photos of her vacations with her parents and sister, childish drawings that her mother lovingly framed, the little bedside light that she made herself at a summer camp, and the old oak desk that her father found at a flea market in Saint-Ouen, and where she sat and studied for all her exams. She's horrified by her reflection in the mirror on the large wardrobe. A few days ago now she decided to take down every mirror in her apartment so that she didn't have to suffer seeing her own image. She eyes her woman's body bitterly, disgusted by her heavy breasts, fat belly, chunky thighs, and dry hands. When did she stop being a little girl and become a woman? She vividly remembers her first period and how anxious she had been when her mother explained that she would bleed down below. She was twelve. It came during a math class. The first pain down there, the first sensation of wet panties, the first sight of that long thread of blood flowing slowly from between her legs into the toilet bowl. She remembers bringing the toilet paper up close after she wiped herself to inspect the red blotches that had seeped into it, the little black clots, running her finger over her vagina to feel the hot cloying blood, first smelling that strong whiff of iron that hung over the restrooms. She waited several days before telling her mother and secretly washed her slacks in the bathroom basin to get rid of the bloodstains. She was ashamed. Filled with a shame that grips women from the start to the very end of their lives. Never changing. Shame for bodies that are imperfect, not spotless, condemned by collective virtue. Bodies that suffer, groan, contort, bleed, change, evolve, grow fatter and thinner, penetrated their whole lives, impregnated, opened, emptied, closed up again, inflated and deflated as a result of successive ordeals, rammed full of acetaminophen and ibuprofen to force them to calm down. Marie knows, she knows that the serene phase of childhood that she now fantasizes about is over. The voice of innocence has fallen silent.

She looks through her bag for the blood pressure monitor that Paul gave her and suddenly feels dizzy. Only slightly but bad enough for her to need to lie down. After resting on her bed for a while she makes up her mind to go back down and rejoin her family. The tall risers of the staircase feel unmanageable. Her feet come down slowly on the carpeted wooden treads, her hand grips the banister and edges gradually downward. She knows she won't fight or call for help. Her head feels heavy, these dizzy spells are getting worse and more frequent, her mind is slipping away. Her body lets itself fall down the huge spiral and crumples on the floor at the foot of the stairs. She was perfectly aware, she could just have sat down or waited a moment and called her husband. The whole family comes running into the corridor. Marie's body is sprawled, almost grotesque. Blood seeps from her forehead, one of her legs is bent out of shape from the fall. "We need to call an ambulance! Quick, quick!" They want to save her. She's not asking for that. All Marie has wanted for months is silence. She's finally achieving her aim, can no longer make out a single sound, but is still dimly aware of what's going on around her. Her husband wants to carry her to the sofa in the living room. Roxane screams at him, whatever they do they mustn't move her before they know what's happened, an internal hemorrhage and it would all be over. They argue, Laurent yells. He's worried about his wife. And about the baby. They must save the child.

⋮

Marie wishes she would never open her eyes again. Her mother's face appears to her more and more clearly. She's gently stroking her hair, telling her to take her time, not try to do anything too quickly. "Don't worry, my darling. Everything's okay, just a broken leg and a cut on your head. The baby's fine, in perfect health. You're safe now." It's still alive. This baby's hanging on, almost surviving its mother, still tarnishing the fibers of its mother's womb, proudly developing while she's dying of misery and pain in this hospital.

Laurent comes into the room, murmurs something, and launches himself at Marie to kiss her. He reeks of alcohol. "I was so scared! When I saw you on the floor I thought I'd die...The baby's fine, it's good and strong, a fighter."

Marie wants to get up but pain shoots up her leg. A blue cast paralyzes part of her right calf. Her whole body is immobilized, pinned to this hard bed. She can't even feel the mattress supporting her or the sheets covering her. She's dead, yet fully alive.

Paul arrives wearing his brightest smile. He gives her positive news about the pregnancy, shows her the ultrasound he did the day before, an x-ray of her leg, and the results of a blood test. Marie wonders whether there's an order of medical priorities in cases like hers. She's in France, a civilized, protective country that guarantees women their right to safety. Not once since her rape and the announcement of her pregnancy has anyone asked her whether she wants to keep this baby. Every pregnant woman should be asked that question at least once during the first gynecological consultation. Conjugal harmony is never adequate to assure genuine happiness or a sincere desire for motherhood. The woman might be under pressure; a wife could be beaten, she could be raped, attacked once or several times, or she could be morally or physically cowed. No one ever really knows what's going on in a woman's mind. Here too, after tumbling downstairs, the first news Marie is given is about her unborn child, not herself. She's simply a womb. The child is prioritized, almost sacred.

"They'll keep you in here another couple of days to be sure everything's okay. In some cases there's a risk of the placenta detaching, so it's better to be cautious. The surgeon who operated on your leg will be here in a few minutes. For now it's rest, rest, rest!"

She won't be able to work at the bank. She's condemned to staying in bed and watching her growing belly all day long, to being absolutely sure she can feel the baby move and come to life inside her free from any danger. There won't be a single distraction now to spare her from thinking about this disaster. Paul wants her to rest. She needs to get her strength back. Her mother and Laurent both kiss her. Roxane and her father stayed outside the room to keep things quiet for when she woke up. Everyone leaves the room and the silence she longed for descends at last. The huge picture window next to her bed is open a little way, letting in a light cool breeze that caresses her face. The windows can be opened only one-quarter of the way. She hears the leaves on the trees shiver under the gray sky, children playing, nurses laughing out loud in the corridor. The ringtone of her cell.

She turns around to reach for her bag and the needle on her drip hurts her; she hates how she feels, tethered by it with every move she makes. She's received a message: "I see you didn't have the courage to speak out. Just like on that wonderful evening together in my car. Keep going like this, in silence, like a good girl, and everything will be fine." He knows. He's proud of her, of her determination to keep it secret. Marie drops the phone. An indescribable anger snaps her awake, constricts her stomach. Her breathing accelerates. He's challenging her with that message, using the word "courage" is like the final victory for his brutality.

Marie rummages in her bag, looking for the pen-knife she bought the day after her rape to be sure she was safe. Now she can use it at last. All those hours practicing in front of the mirror, whipping it out of her coat as quickly as possible to strike her attacker. She grabs it and slides it under the sheets, then removes her panties and slowly inserts the blade between her thighs. She's going to kill this baby, slash this fetus from the inside with all her strength, puncture it, impale it on the blade of her weapon. This is her act of war. During her last scan, she and Laurent could clearly make out its misshapen head, flaccid legs, and distended stomach all floating in amniotic fluid that she hoped was bitter and acidic enough to choke the thing, drown it. This is a real baby she's going to kill, it's not just the little black dot from the early days anymore. She feels the cold blade against the walls of her vagina. Closes her eyes and clenches her teeth. She's going to drive deep into her womb with one sharp thrust, tear her guts by twisting the knife in every direction, to make sure she's done with it once and for all.

Someone knocks at the door. "Hello, I'm Dr. Harcourt. I operated on you this morning and I've come to see how you're doing. My colleague tells me the baby's doing well, which is great news." She discreetly withdraws the penknife. She won't manage it, they won't let her do it. The world is against her. Fortune tips only in the wrong direction, away from what she wants. They all want this baby to be born—well, so be it. Marie accepts her fate. She's exhausted. She gives up on killing her child. It's too late, the moment has passed. She's going to see this pregnancy through to term, supported by her husband, her family, and her friends, who'll pool their efforts to ensure the best possible conditions for her to bring the successful product of her rape into the world. Memories of that night spring up in her mind. She can picture the man, his body oozing pleasure as he came inside her with a long moan that, at the time, seemed to go on forever. Marie doesn't understand why on earth she let the moment slip through her fingers, why she didn't do anything to avoid the worst, why she didn't go to an all-night pharmacy for the morning-after pill and a post-exposure treatment to prevent sexually transmitted diseases such as AIDS, or why she hasn't done a paternity test to be sure about her fate. Instead, she just went home to take a shower and go to bed. It's her own fault. She chose doubt over the truth. She feels ashamed and guilty, thinks how stupid she was not to behave differently. Here in this hospital she's paying a high price, and for once everyone seems to be in agreement with her. The surgeon ends his little spiel with "Do you have any questions?" Not one.

:

Feeling whitish liquid trickling between her legs on Monday evening reminds Marie of her rape. When her blood mingled with her shit and her puke with her blood. The pain pulses through the small of her back, her stomach, arms, and legs. She can feel she's dying. With her hands clenched on the sweat-soaked sheets, her body hovers in the embrace of physical suffering that's impossible to master. The long-forgotten powerful sense of fear resurfaces just as brutally as before. She can't distinguish sounds anymore. A nurse squeezes her hand and encourages her to push even harder. Every contraction tears her body apart. Maybe she'll die on this delivery couch before she even sees her child born. Her pelvis will eventually snap under the pressure. Thirteen hours in labor. It doesn't want to come out. She suddenly regrets forcing this child to come into the world. It didn't ask for anything. If she tells it later that she was raped and didn't have the courage to tell her husband, maybe it won't resent her so much. Its head comes past her perineum. Marie feels like a fucking animal. Paul presses down on her lower abdomen and yells, inserts part of his hand into her vagina to widen the birth canal and help the baby's head through. Her perineum is too tight. "We might need an episiotomy...No, no, scratch that, we're gonna be okay as we are."

People talk in her name, make decisions for her, she has nothing to do but push. Her eyes are wide open. She can hear everything, feel everything. The epidural isn't working, doesn't entirely eliminate the pain. She contemplates the fact that later she'll have to make the decision to kill this baby. She'll wait till Paul and all the nurses have left before she makes her move. She doesn't love it and never will, better for it not to exhaust itself living pointlessly, better for it to go back to where it came from. She's tried to get rid of it before, but that didn't work, she was stopped. There is also a possibility that life will gain the upper hand, that when their eyes meet something will happen and this will stop her strangling it.

The baby gives a heinous scream. Almost before it's been hauled from her gaping vagina, the shapeless bloated creature covered in amniotic fluid, blood, and a waxy white coating is handed to Marie. Its skin is flaky and slightly translucent. She can see its blood vessels in places. It's monstrous. The moist stump of its umbilical cord is stuck to its stomach. Its icy feet paddle gently at her breast. The baby starts opening its eyes but Marie looks away quickly. Its wandering gaze tugs at her emotions. Sticky secretions dribble from its eyes. A green liquid emerges from between its buttocks and spreads over its naked legs. An acidic smell—a vile combination of tar, sweat, and urine—permeates the whole room. Its purplish penis is swollen, distended, almost inflamed. It looks as if the baby's just been raped or beaten up. Marie tries to contain her disgust. The nurse smiles at her idiotically as if to convince her that what's happening right now is a moment of pure pleasure and she should be thrilled that she's extricated this fetus from her fat stomach. "My dear Marie, allow me to introduce your son." You don't introduce a child to its mother. She already knows him better than anyone else. She doesn't have a choice now, she has to look at her son. He's struggling to open his screwed-up little eyes. He writhes in every direction and starts to scream. Marie suddenly feels tired. Her breathing is labored, her eyes slowly close. The baby is taken from her arms, she falls back, lowers her guard, stops fighting. It feels as if her body is emptying itself between her legs. She hears a faraway cry: "Her blood pressure's crashing. She's lost consciousness. Call the crash team in block two." Marie's not frightened. She knows that, once again, everyone will look after her.

．
．
．

We were really scared, you know . . .
When are you going to stop this nonsense!
But you did a good job, just look how
beautiful our son is. Our little Thomas."
Thomas, his grandfather's name. Laurent
is sitting facing her, holding the newborn.
The baby's body is washed, clean and pre-
sentable. Laurent hands him slowly into his
wife's arms. She studies him, analyzes him,
tries to spot the first physical resemblance
to her rapist. She scrutinizes the length of
his hands, his nose, the color of his eyes, his
skin, the shape of his mouth. Everything's
too small. It's too soon, but she's already
convinced that this isn't her husband's
child. Jeanne is sitting next to Laurent and
doesn't share her daughter-in-law's secret

thoughts, judging little Thomas the "spitting image" of Laurent when he was born.

A nurse comes into the room and announces that it's time for a feed. Marie didn't want to breastfeed her son, a decision that unleashed major fights with her husband, who is completely against the idea of formula. In the end she accepted. The child's tiny mouth comes up to Marie's warm breast. Her hands tense, she's frightened. It feels disturbing, perverse: this child, the fruit of her rape as she is convinced he is, sucking her nipple, licking it, pulling it out of shape and squeezing it between his bleeding gums before her husband's and mother-in-law's sentimental eyes. The humiliation is too much. She asks everyone to leave the room so she can be alone with her baby. They comply without asking any questions. Marie's tears roll slowly over the baby's head as he continues to suckle. She's touched by the child's innocence. She feels close to him, suddenly grateful to have carried him inside her through those difficult periods of her life, as if they shared the same ordeal, both victims of the same misfortune. Marie wants to love him. She strokes the blond peach fluff on his tiny head, lifts his little fingers that instinctively grip hers, knowing they're his mother's. Marie won't be able to bear watching Thomas grow up. The newborn of today overwhelms her with emotion, the man of tomorrow terrifies her. A man with a penis, a body, virility, hands stronger than hers, a smell, a voice, a man's future, an animal. If Marie had had a little girl, things would surely have been different. She would have harbored less bitterness toward her. In fact she would have wanted to protect her from everything, to keep her close by her side to spare her from suffering the same torments. It would have become an inner battle. Marie's eyes alight on a large poster stuck to the wall opposite her: "Start your life as a mom in perfect serenity!" Women are offered workshops in relaxation techniques, personal development, discussing their new role as parents and doing pelvic floor exercises to ensure a swift return to sexual activity after childbirth.

Someone knocks at the door. "I'm sorry but I think the baby might need changing. I can show you how to do it if you'd like." Marie uncouples the child from her breast. He regurgitates some of her milk over her and a sour smell wafts up to her face. The nurse carefully takes the baby in her arms, wraps him in a thick blanket and lays him on the changing table next to the bed. Marie doesn't want to see her child naked again. The first sight of his penis horrified her.

Laurent comes in along with his parents and Roxane and her husband. "Oh my God, he's gorgeous! My nephew, little Thomas." Her sister looks at the baby first; her second impulse is to look at Marie. Soon the room will host the whole family, and it will be a carnival for days with permanent comings and goings of friends, relations, and coworkers. Great exclamations about how beautiful the baby is and then incidental congratulations to the mother for doing well. It's not fair being this utterly overlooked. No woman deserves to be treated so badly. A little circle gathers around the baby. Marie, lying in her bed, is excluded. She's merely a spectator. Paul arrives, accompanied by Sophia. Now everyone's here. The story keeps building relentlessly, bringing with it the tension needed to produce the most shocking outcome. The champagne cork pops. Laurent really did think of everything.

∶

Thomas is celebrating his two-
month birthday today. His father hangs a
present on the buggy, a cuddly rabbit toy
that plays a few musical notes while the
baby watches transfixed. The wind blows
and the sky darkens in the space of a few
seconds, sending walkers racing along the
boardwalk that runs the length of the huge
Normandy beach, as they hurry to avoid the
impending storm. Marie adjusts her baby's
top. Through the restaurant's huge picture
window she watches waves break out to
sea. Laurent plays with his son. "I think the
beach can happen tomorrow," he croons.
"His first little walk! My big boy who's two
months old already!" He kisses the baby's
cheek, lifts him slightly to hug him, thrusts

his face right inside the stroller. Marie has stopped noticing his tenderness. She thinks all these demonstrations of affection are misplaced because everything was wrong from the start. A big fat lie grinds away amid all the banality of family life. Laurent's aunt Nathalie, who lives in Deauville all year round, has gone to Martinique for three weeks with her husband and has invited them to come and spend a few days here to make the most of her spacious villa perched high up in the town. Marie would have preferred to stay in Paris, but Laurent, exhausted by his numerous work commitments and his recent appointment to join the company's management team, persuaded her to get away and enjoy the fresh Normandy air.

They're planning to go to Honfleur after their lunch, but right now Thomas needs changing. Marie slips away, so Laurent heads for the restrooms with the baby to change his diaper. The minutes tick by. "They don't have a changing table here. Let's do it in the car instead. Here, you take him and I'll go settle up and join you outside." Marie still holds the baby awkwardly, as if about to drop him. Thomas suddenly howls. His father turns around anxiously, watches his wife from a distance, then turns back to the waiter to pay.

Marie goes out to the car. Every time she has to change the baby's diaper she feels frightened. She doesn't want to see or touch his penis. She peels open the sides of the diaper and rolls it up to throw it swiftly into a plastic bag. She doesn't clean her son's little buttocks with wipes, preferring to look away. But the baby gazes straight at her. Marie lifts his chubby little legs by the feet and fastens the clean diaper. Laurent comes over and checks that everything's okay. He doesn't know why but he always likes to know what his wife is doing. He doesn't suspect her of anything and thinks she's a good mother, but from the start he's felt the need to help and support her in everything she does with the baby.

Marie likes Honfleur, sitting eating waffles with chocolate by the quays that frame and protect the town's small port. When the weather's gray the warm glow of antique shops sheds a weak light over the streets heaving with people. Even in summer Honfleur wears the melancholy of the first days of winter. It is a place that tells the truth. Laurent starts to climb toward the top of town with the stroller while Marie lingers outside the shop fronts of art galleries. A classical-style clay figure of a naked woman slapped by a man catches her eye. She stops for a moment to look at it more closely. Laurent comes up behind her and rests his face in the crook of her neck.

"How poetic. Mind you, sometimes a man's gotta do what a man's gotta do!" He's joking, laughing. All at once the baby cries as if coming to his mother's aid.

They need to get back to the villa soon. Time is constantly counted, divided, subtracted, carved up, torn away from the mother, who must bow to her baby's needs. The day is over.

A large sunbeam breaks through the bedroom curtains. Marie slept badly, the baby woke three times in the night and it was her turn to soothe him. Laurent is still fast asleep next to her. Last night they watched television and drank wine. With his son lying there in his stroller, her husband tried to stroke her between her thighs, to glide his hand over her breasts, but soon realized that nothing would happen. Marie now has absolutely no desire to sleep with her husband; since giving birth her sex drive has completely evaporated. Laurent briefly mentioned the problem to Paul, who advised him to wait awhile, to give his wife some time before resuming normal sexual activity. That's what he's forcing himself to do, but Marie sometimes hears her husband masturbating in bed next to her. She hears him moan, innocently pressing his stiffened penis against her butt, trying gently to spread her thighs, and she sometimes finds traces of semen when she throws back the sheets in the morning. When the tension gets unbearable she consents to perform fellatio or chooses to lie on her stomach so she doesn't have to endure her husband looking at her when he penetrates her.

Laurent gets up and comes to join her in the kitchen. The child is still asleep. Marie is cooking eggs for breakfast. "It's the most fabulous day today. We could go to the beach at the end of the afternoon?" Marie gives a curt nod. She doesn't feel like it. She doesn't feel like anything anymore. She sometimes wonders how long it will take her husband to realize there's something wrong. Maybe he never will. He's burying his head in the sand. He loves his wife with all his heart and doesn't have any suspicions about her despair. She can hide her misery and anger but still struggles to act a part. In a few weeks she'll go back to work at the bank, she can't take being alone with her son all day any longer. In fact she mostly leaves him on his own in his cradle, isolated on the living room carpet or in his bedroom, and makes a point of only feeding and changing him. The bare minimum. At the end of the day his father gives him the ration of affection he needs and that's all he gets.

Laurent dresses Thomas so that the sun can't harm him, and smothers his face and arms with sun cream. Marie attaches the big parasol to the stroller. They're ready to head to the beach. For the first time Laurent's excessive enthusiasm sparks some excitement in Marie at the idea of a family outing. But an inner voice soon reminds her this is just a facade, just another advertising image in which she wants to believe. Marie has given up on bikinis, choosing instead to buy a one-piece swimsuit. She gained twenty-five kilos during her pregnancy and has lost only eight of them. She despises her body. Everything is misshapen. Cellulite on her thighs and buttocks, flaccid skin, sagging breasts, big white stretch marks over her stomach and hips, her vagina still distorted from the birth, her skin dry and damaged by the protracted lack of sleep. She who was so slim, so proud of her smooth slender figure, simply casting off her sarong to skip into the water, now hides behind her towel to take off her slacks and T-shirt. While Laurent stands facing her, undressing insolently. His tanned, muscled body hasn't suffered at all, it's exactly the same as it was fifteen years ago, more beautiful even. "I'm going for a quick swim. I'll be back." A group of young women sitting nearby watches him stride off across the beach. Pitying looks are cast in Marie's direction. What's this fat cow doing with such an attractive man? Marie rummages for candy in the rucksack, stuffs handfuls of colored chocolate balls into her mouth to the sound of mocking laughter. Thomas starts whimpering. His mother hates hearing these first signs of a tantrum, when he ends up dribbling over his clothes and kicking out at the sides of the stroller. She'll have to pick him up. The watching faces suddenly soften. She's a new mother. That explains everything. Her body's changed, which is only natural. The hyenas have vanished, replaced by a charming bouquet of kindly, cooing smiles. "Oh, he's so adorable. How old is he?" Marie snaps her reply, hiding the baby's face with her hand as if to get him away from them, to avoid him enjoying too many compliments.

Laurent returns and Marie hands him the baby so she can go swim. The attention has changed focus: Laurent is now the center of attraction. Marie heads off alone and in silence toward the sea. The water isn't very warm. She quickly wets the back of her neck with her hands, flicks little splashes of cool water over her thighs and stomach, and makes up her mind to dive right in. She swims away, covering quite a distance so she no longer has to hear the shrieks of children playing on the beach. The swell of the waves carries her calmly, sheltered from the frenzy of the shore. Her body feels lighter. She can't remember when she last swam alone. Her limbs stretch out into a cross shape, her head tips back into the water until her ears are completely submerged. The suffering stops for a moment. She wishes she could drift to some unknown space and wake in a different life, not her own. She hears a whistle. She's drifted too far. The lifeguard is waving frantically for her to come back. Marie lifts her head out of the water and starts to swim the breaststroke back toward the shore.

The first steps she takes on the beach are shameful. She is almost scolded, reprimanded. She looks for their parasol but can't see it. And yet she was sure they set up camp not far from the showers. She keeps walking and spots the group of young women who were watching her earlier. They're sitting on the sand with their long legs stretched out, forming a circle around Laurent and Thomas. The one with the blond hair and tanned skin can't be more than twenty years old. She's sitting next to Marie's husband, hooting, roaring with laughter, watched by her friends and a smiling Laurent. "Everything okay?" Marie asks. "Am I disturbing you?" Laurent looks up at his wife and asks whether she had a nice swim. The women move away. Marie's towel, which was being used to sit on, is impregnated with sand. She snatches it up to shake it and grains of sand fly in every direction. "Stop that, can't you see you're getting it right in his eyes?" She keeps shaking. Laurent grabs her arm forcefully and she eventually stops. Laurent puts the baby in his stroller, still eyeing his wife with furious bafflement. She ignores his anger, turns to look the other way. They decide to leave. Some way away, the women wave discreetly to Laurent. The baby cries, he's hungry. They must get back to the villa quickly.

Tomorrow their vacation will be over. Marie is returning to work at the bank, reunited with her co-workers and clients. The baby will be in a day nursery until his mother picks him up in the evening. Laurent is driving quickly. He turns to Marie with a smile. "It's a long time since I've seen a little jealous outburst…I actually kind of like it…" His hand moves from the gearshift onto his wife's thigh. Marie feels like slapping his face but in the end opts to put her hand over his so as not to exhaust herself with another fight. This physical connection between husband and wife is the first in some time. Thomas grizzles a little on the rear seat, then suddenly gives a long piercing cry that fills the whole car. His parents are surprised; it's the first time he's done this. Laurent watches him tenderly in the rearview mirror. Marie turns around to look at him, stares at him for a moment: "Like father, like son."

The baby is in terrible pain. He howls on the examination table, kicks out energetically, and scratches with all his strength at the small mattress on which he's lying. Marie is wearing a beautiful dress, cinched at the waist, Laurent a perfectly tailored suit. From the start of the appointment the pediatrician was struck by the couple's perfect appearance. "It's still not a pretty sight but it's better than last time. The treatment is working well and the infection in his penis is gradually going down. He was lucky, it could have been a lot more serious." Laurent is very attentive, hanging on the doctor's every word, studying every detail of his face. He's afraid he may miss one of his instructions. Marie gazes out the window, then briefly rejoins the conversation. She knows it's her fault, but doesn't really feel involved in what's happening to her son.

Laurent has been completely swamped by work for three weeks. He's been coming back to the apartment late at night and Marie has had to delay her return to work once again so that she can stay with Thomas until they find a place in a day nursery. They put in their application well in advance, but September was already over and the other new parents were several weeks ahead of them on waiting lists. Marie had to look after her son single-handed for days on end. She didn't wash him every day, changed his diaper only rarely, and camouflaged the unpleasant smell of soured milk in the folds of his neck with baby perfume. When Laurent arrived home at around nine he found his son asleep in his cradle, giving off a pleasant smell of lavender cream. He kissed him on the forehead and set off for work again at seven the next morning.

Last Saturday evening Marie was having dinner in a restaurant with Sophia. Glad to be spending some time alone with his son at last, Laurent stayed at home to look after him. Before Marie left, she told him she'd already changed and fed the baby. At about ten o'clock Laurent heard Thomas cry, almost choking. He was burning up with fever, sweating, his clammy wet skin shifting from red to gray. His eyes closed slowly and his breathing grew increasingly halting. Laurent called his wife immediately and left a message telling her to meet him in the emergency room as soon as possible. Marie didn't get there until midnight; she'd turned off her cell. The pediatrician's diagnosis was incontrovertible: "This is clearly a case of neglect. Your child hasn't been washed or changed properly for weeks. I'd say easily a month. The infection started in the anal canal. On examination I found a significant anal fistula that will require a course of antibiotics. His penis is also beginning to succumb to infection because it hasn't been washed or had the foreskin drawn back. I would say he has balanoposthitis, an inflammation of the glans and foreskin that we'll try to treat with drugs in the first instance."

The word "neglect" smacked Laurent full in the chest. He struggled to stay upright on his chair, stunned by the situation. His cell phone rang, it was Marie, who'd just arrived at the hospital. He thanked the doctor, assured him he would follow his advice to the letter, would be very careful, they were just tired new parents with no experience, still not entirely used to looking after a baby. The pediatrician understood, asked him to be careful and vigilant. He printed out several prescriptions and set an appointment for the following week to see how the treatment was going.

The click of high heels rang out in the corridor and a breathless Marie arrived. "Is it over already? I'm so sorry, I ran out of battery and then I went home...There was nobody there, I was scared. What did the doctors say? What's wrong with him?" Marie's panicky words sounded hollow. She leaned in toward her baby but Laurent turned the stroller away, said Thomas was very tired and they should go home. On the way home he sat in silence, his hands gripping the steering wheel. Marie had had a good deal to drink, she and Sophia had done a lot of laughing. She was relaxed, enthusiastic, she didn't want to come back down from her emotional high into the drab and restrictive family life she'd been subjected to for months.

Laurent didn't know how to broach the subject with his wife; then, infuriated by her inappropriate calm, he eventually launched his offensive: "We need to find a place in a day nursery real soon. Things can't go on like this, Marie. Not for you or for Thomas, or even for me. Do you get what just happened? The doctor basically called us unfit parents. He used the word 'neglect.' I don't know if you understand what that means. Parental neglect is really serious."

Marie thought he was overdoing it. Well, she'd been exhausted the last few weeks, but then she was the one looking after their son full-time. She was the one who gave up her career for the sake of her husband's, staying at home with her son every weekday with no help. And now he was calling her an unfit mother because she didn't change a diaper right and she didn't keep cleaning dribbles of milk off his neck.

Confronted with his wife's rebuke, Laurent was placated, he understood. He knew she was very tired with the new routine, that she thought it was unfair she couldn't work like him. He kissed her, forgave her, promised to find a solution the very next day even if that meant hiring a nanny to help her. Over the next few days Laurent came home from work earlier.

Her colleagues asked her to bring the baby into the office. They're waiting expectantly to welcome her outside the bank. Marie had no desire whatsoever to show off her son to everyone; keeping her career and her family life separate has been her only source of comfort in the last few months. But they insisted and she didn't feel able to refuse. Her office, which used to be clean, neutral, and tidy, is littered with a multitude of little niceties and gifts sent by her most loyal clients. "And look...Even Laurent helped us." Hervé hands Marie a small gilded frame holding a photograph of her, Laurent, and Thomas in the hospital's maternity unit. She remembers the moment very clearly. Her heart breaks. It's six thirty in the evening, the end of the day, and her coworkers have organized a little drink to celebrate her imminent return. "Things have changed a bit, you know. Janine left, Xavier took over Patrice's job..." She listens but is already swamped by the tide of information she's given. Little Thomas is handed around from one person to the next.

Marie feels as if she is having her period, her pants feel wet. She entrusts her son to her manager's care and slips away to the restroom. After the exhaustion of her pregnancy, she and Laurent would rather wait before conceiving a second child. Marie doesn't want one, anyway; she went back on the pill as soon as Thomas arrived. She thinks how quickly everything changed. A day, an hour, the last moment before her rape, she could see herself living with Laurent and their four children. They would have moved into a larger apartment in Paris, maybe even a small house. Laurent is now earning a lot, everything would have been possible. She doesn't have her period yet, just a feeling. "But really, going back to work after just a few months...She just doesn't want to look after her kid. With my first I stayed at home for two and a half years to bring him up. But she and her husband must be planning to have a nanny so they have no problem! I tell you, some women..." Marie doesn't recognize the voice. The two women are talking next to the washbasins, criticizing her for coming back to work so soon. They think she'll be out of her depth with the new business model, that she's already a little too old to achieve her goals. Marie feels tears pricking her eyes, her throat constricts. She doesn't have the courage to come out of the stall to confront the women and chooses instead to wait till they've left.

When she rejoins her coworkers Thomas is still bouncing on her manager's knee. Marie needs to leave, she wants to be on form tomorrow and to use the weekend to study her files. Hervé hands her a large file in which he's arranged printouts of up-to-date information on all her best clients. "So you'll know exactly where you stand on Monday without any panic." She's touched by his kindness. His genuine smile, the awkward way he always has his arms crossed, his too-big suits, his nervous little laugh, his colorful Disney ties; if he were her husband he'd understand her better than anyone, she's sure of it.

When she's back at the apartment Laurent calls to tell her not to wait up, he's having dinner with his boss to discuss an important new case. The baby's lying on his playmat. She doesn't look at him and starts heating some noodles left over from yesterday. Thomas cries, he's hungry. When he was tiny she always delayed his feeds, constantly balking at being forced to breastfeed him. Laurent eventually noticed this after a few months. Since the baby's infection she needs to be vigilant. She came up with the idea of expressing her milk and making up bottles in advance. Thomas can wait till she's finished her noodles this evening, then she'll take the bottle from the fridge. She sits on the kitchen counter and watches the baby crawling on the floor. He's very agile for his age. In fact the pediatrician said he was clever and alert. She finishes her meal and goes over to the baby with the bottle in her hand. When she has him in her arms she tries not to make eye contact for too long. She's aware of his smell, would like to stroke him, kiss his forehead, whisper sweet nothings in his ears. But she can't. She can't get her rapist's face out of her mind. She settles for supporting Thomas so that he can finish his milk as quickly as possible and can then go to bed. Before, she didn't even take the time to burp him but she now feels she has to. She doesn't want to risk him choking, a danger that had never occurred to her before the doctor mentioned it.

Laurent comes home from work and she regrets that she's not asleep. Pumped up by alcohol and the new case, he'll try to touch her again. She can't pretend anymore and wishes she could tell him to find another solution to satisfy his sexual needs. The last time they had sex was two months ago. She let him have his way. Penetrated by her husband for many long minutes, waiting for him to finish. But he was particularly active that evening, turning her in every direction like a sack of potatoes, stuffing his fingers in her mouth, muttering dirty talk in her ear. He ejaculated over her stomach, pulling out at the last minute as if afraid of coming inside her.

Laurent tiptoes into the room, undresses, and lies down next to her. There's a strong smell of whiskey on his breath. He presses his erection up against her buttocks, slowly rocking his hips. Marie grunts, asks him to let her sleep. He slips his hands between her thighs. She moves away. Laurent gives up, gets out of bed, and leaves the room. He seems annoyed but she doesn't take much interest.

Many long minutes later he hasn't come back to bed. The alarm clock on the nightstand says two thirty. Marie gets up to see what her husband's doing. There's a dim light on in the living room. She walks along the corridor past the front door without a sound. Laurent is sitting on the sofa with his laptop on his knee. She can't see the scene very clearly, there isn't enough light. She steps silently closer behind him, hears the sounds, understands. Laurent pants, gasps, masturbating over porn: a girl taken by two men. He sighs, his erect penis in his hand. His legs are spread, his head resting on the back of the sofa. Marie watches him, frozen behind him, slightly shocked. Laurent's no different from any other man, he never has been. He's just a man who wants to have his wife whenever he feels like it. "The woman is passive as a toilet, for the man to do his business in." This sentence from the writer Elfriede Jelinek suddenly comes back to her. She was lent the book *Lust* years before she was raped. She remembers not finishing it. She found it shocking, unfair, disgusting, particularly that sentence. A stupid feminist bitch. Things are different now. Marie wants to wait to see her husband come over his porn film. She wants to know if he'll be the same as when they're together. After all, she didn't know many men before him. He gives a restrained little cry. Semen spurts over his stomach, his penis still erect in his hand. The laptop slides onto the sofa next to him. The video continues. She watches the images of the girl dressed in school uniform and covered in semen, kneeling before two huge penises that strain in front of her face. Marie creeps away without her husband noticing her. She buries herself under the covers. She can feel her vagina is swollen, wet, hot. She squeezes her legs together, refuses to experience any arousal after what she's just seen. Her body arches. She puts her hand inside her panties, slowly strokes her clitoris. Marie has succumbed but she's alone at last. He won't come now.

:

On the last Saturday before Marie goes back to work she's bubbly with happiness, she's almost forgotten the incident the night before. Laurent comes into the kitchen with his eyes barely open. "I slept really badly last night, I'm going back to bed soon." Marie keeps stirring the scrambled eggs in the pan. The baby has been very placid for a few days and he's just slept through the night for the first time. It's Laurent's turn to give him his bottle this morning. A relief for Marie. She can't get used to looking after her child.

"Baptiste gave me a new case yesterday. Kind of complicated, I'm not sure I'll take it." Marie likes it when her husband tells her about his current clients. Probate cases are often boring, divorces are more titillating. "It's a media magnate. His wife wants a divorce but the problem is she's accusing him of raping a minor. Apparently he got a little too close to one of his daughter's friends. Thirteen, I mean really..." This is the second time their paths have crossed on the same word. Last time was with Paul. Marie doesn't say anything, lets him keep talking: "But nothing's been proved yet. I think it's something his wife cooked up to get a fatter settlement out of him. The mother of the girl is a really good friend of hers. I don't know...You should see him, he doesn't look like someone who'd do that sort of thing."

That sort of thing. She thinks of her CEO. He doesn't really look like a rapist either.

"So what do you think they *do* look like, guys who rape women? Do they have bleeding vaginas tattooed on their shoulders or wear swastikas around their necks?" Surprised by her aggressive remark, Laurent instinctively looks up from his cup of coffee. Marie is shocked by her own words. She didn't think. She turns away, suddenly regretting letting herself get carried away. She needs to focus now, think about what she says next, not awaken any suspicion. She tempers her words, rephrases them to moderate their impact, smiles at her husband, spoons the eggs onto the plate, ends up changing the subject. He's stopped listening. Has already forgotten.

As she works her way up and down the supermarket aisles with her stroller, Marie can't help thinking over what she said this morning about Laurent's client. She thinks he's going to start realizing something. The shelves of vitamins and food supplements are laden with hundreds of boxes in all shapes and sizes. Marie desperately wants to lose her excess weight, be back to the slim attractive woman she was before her pregnancy. An older lady next to her coos over Thomas. Marie knows that he finds new fans every time they go out. The questions, always the same: how old he is, whether he's sleeping through the night... There are about ten women in the health and vitamin aisle. Most of them are overweight, lingering over boxes of diet pills, shamelessly grabbing big pots of protein powder and tossing packets of low-calorie meal replacement bars into their carts. Marie is a little skeptical and wonders whether these products really work. She's ashamed to be in this part of the supermarket. Before having her baby she wouldn't have hung around here for a moment, she would even have made fun of these poor lazy, overweight women who may still hope their husbands will find them attractive when they come home from work. Marie scours the displays, drifts from one end of the shelves to the other. She doesn't know which brand to choose, tries to find her shopping list. Nothing.

She suddenly realizes she left her purse by the door when she took a basket. She runs over to the check-out counters, racing through the displays of vegetables, terrified she's had everything stolen. "Excuse me, did you see a purse? I left it near the door by mistake. It's red leather." The security guard looks at her without a word, pivots slightly, and takes Marie's purse from a plastic tray. She's relieved. It would have been unbearable to lose her things, her appointment book and her cell just two days before going back to work. She heads slowly back through the shop with the strap of her purse safely over her shoulder.

As she stands in line at the first checkout, she catches the eye of the older lady who stopped to make a fuss over Thomas. The baby. She forgot the baby. Her eyes open wide, her stomach clenches, the floor beneath her feet distorts. She sets off, running, panicking, breathless, looking for the stroller and her child. Everyone watches her, curious. She reaches the health section, where she left Thomas. There's no stroller. A huge wave of terror sweeps over her. She races up and down every aisle, jumps from one place to the next, spins in every direction, starts to scream. A member of staff notices her and asks what's going on. "I lost my baby! I don't know, I was gone a couple of seconds and the stroller's not there. A gray stroller. Help me please!" The young girl, who seems to be just a trainee, sets off quickly toward the checkout counters.

Noticing Marie's and the girl's alarm, the customers standing in line start listening to find out what's causing their agitation. The trainee grabs the mic in front of a helpless cashier. "Your attention please. A mother is looking for her baby who was in the store a few minutes ago. If you see a gray stroller, please come to the checkout counters immediately. Please, this is an emergency. I repeat, a mother's looking for her baby..." Marie's legs threaten to give way. If she doesn't find Thomas, Laurent will never forgive her for being so negligent.

Once the announcement has been made the cashier goes back to scanning items. Life goes on. The store manager arrives. "I heard the announcement, we can call the police if you'd like us to..." Marie doesn't know, is lost. Some employees take hold of her. She's paralyzed, destroyed, in a state of shock, her arms dangling empty, her shoulders slumping down over her breasts. Maybe yes. Maybe no. She needs to decide, time is ticking by. They'll send out a report of an abduction. Laurent's bound to hear about it on TV. She's about to follow the manager to his office when she hears someone cry: "He's here! The baby's here, I'm with him." Marie turns around. A tall blond fifty-something woman has come to the checkout counters with the stroller. She waves her arms. Marie stays rooted to the spot for a few seconds before running over to her. She hugs the woman, thanks her with all her heart, babbles the same words two or three times in succession. After a few explanations of her sudden disappearance, Marie takes the stroller back. Only five minutes have passed. Every customer in the store is staring at her. Some whisper as she passes. People eye her with disgust, horror. Ashamed, she decides to leave, gives up on the shopping.

On the way home Thomas smiles at his mother. "I nearly lost you today...I nearly lost you." She finds these words a strange sort of relief, they break the silence between her and her son. She doesn't normally speak to him, preferring to establish enough distance so that they don't run the risk of becoming attached to each other.

Laurent is still in his pajamas on the sofa, working on his laptop. He turns around to look at his wife, amazed. "Are you okay? Why didn't you do the shopping?" Marie puts her things down in the hall to give herself time to think about her reply. "No, the Charonne supermarket was closed today. I'll go to the one in Bastille this evening." Laurent gets up to lift Thomas from the stroller. He kisses him and sniffs his diaper. "Aha, he needs changing." Marie knows he does but she's already on her way to the bedroom to look through the notes Hervé prepared for her. Monday is a big day. She's going back to work at last, Thomas is going to the day nursery and Laurent is starting his defense on a new case. Everything will be just like before.

∙
∙
∙

Marie likes dropping off her son at the day nursery. She has a pleasant feeling of being rid of him. The child-care workers instantly take charge of Thomas, exchange a few words with her, and let her leave for work with her hands free, relieved of the heavy burden that he represents for her. Unlike the other mothers who feel guilty and smother their babies with kisses before going, Marie leaves as promptly as she arrives. "I'm running late": her favorite phrase in the morning. Little Thomas gets farther and farther from his mother's arms, watching her as she walks off down the corridor. She's gone.

The last time Marie came to the bank was for the drink that her coworkers arranged in Thomas's honor. No one's waiting for her on the doorstep now. On her previous visit she already noticed some changes: coffee machines in the clients' waiting area, large sofas instead of rigid plastic chairs, tall glass panels replacing the doors on all the offices, a large space that was previously enclosed adapted into an open-plan area for seeing student clients. In the space of a few months the bank has decided to modernize.

Hervé comes over to Marie to give her a coffee. "So, it's the big day. Not too stressed?" Some way away two young women stand watching them and giggling. Marie turns to stare at them. "Ah yes, they're new. We now have to work in pairs on some files…You see, there's a policy of cooperation between the old guard and the young. Transferring skills." She's not old, only thirty-two, and she's already being asked to play the part of someone overtaken by technology and ignorant of the codes used by "the young." Anyway, her clients are old too. Old and rich with capital and shareholdings. The bank's younger clients are usually broke, overdrawn by the end of every month, staying for years on end with their entry-level accounts that allow them only a debit card, and usually overseen by a lowly account adviser over the phone or on the Internet.

Marie knows that the early weeks will be difficult. When she goes into her office the glass door bothers her: she feels watched, maliciously spied on. Everyone else seems used to it. Her email in-box has a couple of reminders from human resources about her return to work, some administrative forms to fill out. Her finger rolls over the wheel on the mouse, scrolling through her messages. She stops. He's dared to make contact again: "We all wish Marie a smooth first day back today!" The CEO's email is copied to everyone in the whole branch. Her hands hover over the keyboard, and she fights to get a grip of herself. She immediately deletes the message.

A young woman barges into her office without knocking. She has a pile of multicolored files in her arms and sets them down on Marie's desk. "Hi, I'm Mathilde, the new international business trainee? We're working together on the real estate files. Here are the docs. If you like we could grab lunch sometime this week to check out some details and get to know each other?"

Marie finds her turn of phrase unsettling but doesn't let it show. She's disturbed by the girl's affected Lolita vibe. Her pneumatic backside, firm breasts, and flawless white skin, and her smell of raspberries and peaches. Marie remembers the porn film her husband was watching when she saw him masturbating. This girl would perfectly match the selection criteria. She suddenly feels a twinge of jealousy. In a relaxed, natural tone of voice, Marie accepts Mathilde's suggestion for lunch, then asks her to forgive her but she's expecting her first meeting shortly.

She knows Monsieur Geignard very well; he's an old client who's retired and enjoys playing the stock market. Marie opens her client files program. An error message pops up. She tries again. Same thing. She gets up to ask Hervé what's going on, but he's already in a meeting.

"You okay? Is something wrong?" From Lolita. Although uncomfortable at the thought of being given advice by someone barely out of her teens, Marie eventually explains her problem. "Oh yes, they said you used H-five, but all the banks moved on to H-six some time ago now. That old stuff was super-slow. But it's no big deal, I'll show you how it works." How could the bank make this change so abruptly without keeping the old version in place and giving its employees time to adapt to the transition? Mathilde comes into her office with her. Marie feels handicapped, helped in everything she does, overtaken by the speed of technological change, with no training or experience, ready to be thrown in the trash. A little old lady of thirty-two steered by advice from a twenty-two-year-old.

Marie will spend the entire day relying on the help of her coworkers. After her long months of maternity leave she can't even handle herself on her own.

Tonight they're watching a movie and going to bed early. "How did your first day at work go?" Marie lies, not wanting to lose credibility with her husband on the professional front. Line 9 of the Métro was down so she decided to take the bus for the first time in ages, but when it stopped to pick up some regulars she turned away and decided to walk. On the way home it came to her in a flash: she could drop everything. She would just leave an explanatory note for her husband and son, escape to the station or the airport in a taxi and leave with just a couple of suitcases. She knows she won't manage to kill herself for now. Suicide needs a single moment of real courage. She's not capable of it.

As she sits sweetly next to her husband, it suddenly strikes her she's the perfect embodiment of what society most despises: a fat, weak, cowardly woman who doesn't love her child, is contemplating leaving her family, and is sexually underactive, inefficient and incompetent at work, and already old. An ad for toilet paper comes on, carried along by the brisk lilt of a Wagner melody. A woman rubs her face with a piece of the pink paper to show viewers just how soft and nice it is. All at once an aura lights up her body and lifts it into a turquoise-blue sky scattered with big white clouds, then scrolls softly around a colorful bouquet of flowers. Marie sighs. Laurent opens the packet of potato chips on his knees. "Seriously, Wagner for a toilet paper ad? They could do better."

The movie starts. She insisted on watching her favorite film, *All about Eve*, simply to witness for the hundredth time Bette Davis's masterly performance. A woman she's always aspired to resemble: beautiful, powerful, honest, passionate, loving, spirited, arrogant, hysterical, melancholy, and sensitive all at once. Margo Channing is *the* woman, a unique character who'll never age. Marie is totally captivated by the movie. Laurent fills his face with potato chips dipped in a bowl of guacamole. He wanted to make his wife happy. *It's obvious you're not a woman.* That line pierces Marie's heart. Her hands tense, tears spill down her cheeks. She feels as if the scene is being played out for her. "She really is kind of hysterical...Poor guy." What men like Marie's husband want most of all is peace and quiet. The poor man, the poor husband disoriented by his wife's scenes when she's trying to assert herself as she is and as she sees fit. With her mind, her body, and her voice. They like taking their wives in hand while still leaving them a small margin of freedom so they have access to modern amusements, such as work or "a drink with the girls." The power that a husband has over his wife is hidden, even inverted. A woman who's given her freedom suddenly finds it unjustified, delights in occasionally backpedaling into the sweet comfort of dependence.

The trap closes in. The movie is over. They head to bed without any commentary. There's nothing they need to say.

He snores. She's awake, staring at the bedroom door. It has a lock. She's never thought of locking the doors in the apartment. Everything's open like the glass offices at the bank. She's always being disturbed and never has time to think. Even in bed there's her husband grunting next to her. The baby's been howling for the last ten minutes. Laurent's only just stirring, clumsily pats his wife's shoulder for her to get up. It's her turn today. Oh, the agony of getting up! Thomas is almost naked in his cot, his sleepsuit thrown on the floor. Marie picks up his things to dress him, then feeds his little hands through the sleeves, holding his head to keep him still. He scratches her breast and kicks her in the chin. She immediately lets go of him, flinging him back against the cushioning. He cries again but his mother doesn't regret her reaction. She just wants him to stop. She wraps him in the tartan blanket that Irene knitted for him last month and wanders up and down the corridor rocking him for a long time, shaking him. She hates being alone with her son. All the lights are out in the building opposite. It's three a.m. The boulevard Voltaire is silent, with just a few scooters still passing under the yellow glow of the streetlights.

Marie wants to make the most of the quiet and goes over to the balcony. It was the one thing she insisted on when they were looking for an apartment. She wanted a terrace or balcony so she could have her coffee outside in the summer. She opens the French window and a cold draft whisks over her, startling Thomas. She walks forward with the baby in her arms. She peers down. The balconies are wide but deserted. She looks at her son and he smiles at her. The sky is black. The metal shutters are down on all the shops, life will begin again tomorrow. But what form will it take? The same as ever, inevitably. She loosens the blanket and throws it to the floor, slowly puts her foot on the first metal bar of the balustrade. Her body rises slightly. Thomas is quiet, fingering the buttons on his mother's pajamas. She holds him standing up on the ledge. Fourth floor. He'll crash to the ground without making too much noise. His little bones will snap in a split second and his flesh will break away instantly from the violence of the impact. He won't suffer but his mother will just have to look away from her child's corpse. Then Marie could go downstairs and run away with no risk of turning back. She wants it to be over with and to throw him out now. Half hanging over the void, she gives him a series of shy little nudges so that he slides slowly. Eventually she closes her eyes. She has her hands flat over his round stomach still full of warm milk.

There's a sound behind her. Her husband calls. Marie opens her eyes. She snatches the child back into her arms and picks up the blanket to wrap it around him. Laurent is now on the far side of the living room. He freezes for a moment, watching his wife from a distance. "What the hell are you doing outside? Are you nuts? Thomas will catch cold, come inside!" He runs over to them and wants to take the baby, but Marie jerks away from him.

"Leave me alone! I just wanted some fresh air, I'm still allowed to breathe, aren't I, or is that forbidden too?" Laurent doesn't know what to do. Maybe since Thomas's infection he's been too domineering with Marie, making her feel guilty about anything and everything. She strides angrily back to Thomas's bedroom to put the baby in his cot.

Laurent apologizes for being angry, he didn't mean to upset her. "I know you're a good mother, but I sometimes get the feeling something's changed. We don't really talk much anymore. I know you'll tell me I'm very busy at work, but you know..." Marie has stopped listening. His words flit past her. She regrets her cowardice, never managing to stay the course. She can't bear her own weakness, her inability to see things through, those tiny microseconds that would have been enough for her to push her child off the ledge, then climb over it herself or just go downstairs and run away. Instead she's stuck back in this bed again. The same bed in which she took refuge after her rape.

Laurent touches her breast. He wants a reconciliation. He wants peace. He thinks sex is the only proof of true happiness. Marie lets him have his way. Yes, let him get on with it. Let him fuck her however he wants to, in every hole if need be, and afterward he'll forget his suspicions about his wife. He'll forget the lurking fear he felt at the thought of her throwing his son from the fourth floor. Because he knows deep down: there's a problem. Something that he can't quite pin down and that he refuses to see or acknowledge. The light is on. The husband likes to see his wife when he penetrates her. Keeps switching back on the light that his wife battles to turn off so she doesn't have to witness her own humiliation. He puts his hands on her hips, strokes her stomach, spreads her legs, then goes down toward her vagina. His sexual desire disgusts her. She willfully tries to stay dry between her legs. She struggles desperately to sustain the tragedy of those few seconds when she wanted to kill her son, in order to suppress the sick sexual impulses deep inside her. She turns around and kisses him. Laurent is surprised. From murder to love, from semen to blood, from lust to death, it's her flesh that dictates to her. Exhausted, penetrated, and in pain, aching from the physicality of Laurent's body moving on top of hers, Marie pants like a good little bitch. What's the point of peace when all it does is feed the hate. There's no chance left for harmony or mollification between Laurent and Marie, no rest and precious little common sense. She pays. She gives. She sucks. And if there's to be no truce she'd rather have the acknowledged violence of war than the weakness of a quiet life. In a final flash of consciousness before she falls asleep the word "wife" comes to her at last.

:

Marie doesn't want to pick little Thomas up from the day nursery. She's taken a day off work specifically to be alone and so she can enjoy the shops in the morning. She did some research on the Internet last night with a view to buying some sexy lingerie. In spite of her full hips and the fact that she loathes her body since her pregnancy, she finally feels able to make an effort for Laurent, and their last sexual interaction has encouraged her to be more passionate. She'd like to surprise him. When he comes home from work she'll be waiting for him on the sofa in the living room dressed only in her matching underwear, a glass of champagne in her hand. She'll saunter sensuously over to him to whisper a few dirty words. They'll be happy again. They'll forget.

When she arrives outside the shop on the rue des Orfèvres, she stands transfixed in front of the window display for a moment. The mannequins showing off the lingerie are very slim. She's fat, she'll never be able to get even one of her legs into those G-strings. She takes a deep breath and makes up her mind to go in. A sales assistant comes straight over to her to offer her help. "Hi. I'm looking for a matching set. Something chic and sexy." She suddenly feels unsure. Bearing in mind the porn films Laurent likes, she's not convinced that the combination of "chic and sexy" features in her husband's fantasies, or the fantasies of men in general. The sales assistant shows her two sets in black-and-purple lace. Marie shakes her head and tries to find her cell phone, claiming there's an emergency. She apologizes, says she'll come back later. Laurent wouldn't be turned on by chic lingerie.

She takes the Métro again and heads for Pigalle in the north of Paris. Tourists like strolling along the wide avenues in the Eighteenth Arrondissement, drifting toward the shops up at Montmartre and sampling the big brasseries. Marie has never thought of living in this neighborhood, this isn't the sort of bustle she enjoys. The boulevard de Clichy isn't very busy at ten in the morning but a few regulars at the big Video X Club movie theater are already hanging around outside, waiting impatiently for the start of the first screening. Marie knows she won't meet anyone she knows in this part of Paris. She doesn't feel like going into the Sexodrome, the huge sex supermarket on the corner. She'd prefer somewhere smaller, more intimate. The sign over Hot Pussy a little farther up the boulevard beckons to her. Large red drapes dotted with sequins hang over the doorway, which looks like the entrance to a cabaret rather than a sex shop. She peers furtively between the gaps in the drapes and sees two women chatting next to the checkout. They look friendly enough. Marie decides to go in, and a shrill bell like something from a dusty provincial hardware store announces her arrival to the sales assistants. A prolonged silence descends. With her dainty patent leather loafers, designer handbag, and sport-chic blouse, Marie doesn't really look like the usual clientele. She wants to turn back, but one of the girls comes over to her as if greeting the First Lady.

"Good morning, madame. May I help you?"

Marie is aware of the carefully chosen words and opts to be equally polite: "Hello, yes. You see, I'd like to buy a little schoolgirl outfit." Another silence. "And if possible, something all one color."

The assistant asks Marie to follow her down to the basement where there are hundreds of outfits on hangers. "We have a lot of choice in school uniforms. We have red, blue, or green kilts. So there's a wide choice, but if you don't mind my saying, the red would suit you very well." Marie is flattered. Along the side of the large basement she notices a small recess in red stone, lit with green and pink neon lights. The assistant explains that this is where the video booths and the peep show are. Intrigued, Marie asks what she means. "A girl dances in a booth and men watch from the other side. We just show porn films in the other booths."

Marie has a sudden revelation about how simple male sexuality is, how little depth there is to it. With these objectified women dancing naked in a cage, these porn films featuring eager little school girls, these nurse's uniforms, policewoman uniforms, gift-wrapped-with-a-bow outfits, dresses, skirts, stockings, vinyl...She's standing facing a whole walk-in closet that reflects what most men want from sex. Reproducing what appeals to them from the porn films they watch or in the sexy ads on the Internet, featuring—in ninety-nine percent of cases—a girl who's not entirely naked. The fantasy of a body free of any artifice arouses men but doesn't necessarily make them want sex right away. Men like to feel they get a hard-on quickly, they find it reassuring. Everything leads back to her rape. Sex, violence, submission, pornography. Marie's never thought to look for an explanation for the attack. Here in this sex shop, surrounded by all these accessories intended chiefly for men's pleasure, she wonders furiously how many men in the world are raping women right now. The sort who abuse with no regrets. Her eye rests momentarily on a little old man emerging from one of the booths. He looks away with the slight hangdog disappointment of someone who's fun is over now. Marie pities him. All the unpleasant associations fall apart. She can't think straight, no longer sees the subtleties, has muddle-headed theories. Holding the schoolgirl outfit in her hand, she comes back to her senses. "Well then, I'll take this one. Where can I try it on?" The assistant explains with some embarrassment that there are only three sizes and that she can't try the clothes on without buying them afterward. Marie takes the medium. The miniskirt is bound to be a little tight but she refuses to go up to a large for now. It's psychological.

Back up on street level the other assistant, a chunky brunette poured into too-tight low-rise jeans, offers her the accessories that go with her outfit: schoolgirl glasses, a phallus-shaped lollipop, short white socks, a red hair ribbon, and a tartan vibrator. Marie takes the lollipop and the hair ribbon. The two salesgirls thank her for her visit and offer her a loyalty card that they stamp with the name Hot Pussy so that she can have a discount next time. Marie is pleased with what she's bought but asks not to have a branded bag, so they hand her a large opaque black bag with no logo.

Once she's home, Marie wants to try on the little outfit she's bought, but first she needs to do her makeup. She's never changed her ways: she always looks natural and sensible but this evening she wants to be someone different, to look like a slut for her husband. Black around her eyes, her mouth screaming red, her skin tone more orange than usual, her hair tied back with the red ribbon. Now she takes the black bag from the bed and takes out her acquisitions. The cropped top just about works, but her full breasts end up slipping down onto her stomach and there are stretch marks everywhere, indelible signs of her tragedy. The skirt is more difficult to put on and the love handles on her hips partly hide the belt. She looks like a fat pig or a transvestite, but definitely not the pretty schoolgirl in her husband's film. In a last attempt at getting the look, she puts on the tie that goes with the top. She inspects her reflection in the full-length mirror and feels ridiculous, standing there like a great heavy lump. She doesn't know why she had this stupid idea about a costume. Like other women her age, she should have stayed in the realm of sexy chic. Bulging out of the outfit, she struggles to undo the costume but has to lie flat on her back on the bed to reach all the buttons. She rolls over, battling with the scraps of fabric. The golden heart clasp on the belt pops off and lands on the carpet, and the lacing on the skirt tears with the pressure from her fat body.

All at once she hears a key turn in the lock on the front door. She freezes. She's not expecting anyone. She leaps up from the bed but trips because of the too-tight skirt with its attached garter belt. The door slams and she hears Laurent's voice. She scrambles over the floor and eventually manages to slough off part of the outfit. She reaches furtively for her robe in the bathroom to go and join her husband. Laurent is opening a tray of sushi on the coffee table in the living room. A woman is talking to him with her back to him as she pulls a few books from the shelves. Marie announces her presence with a little cough. Laurent turns around, his mouth full of sushi. His eyes register horror. Total silence in the room. He doesn't recognize her.

"Marie? What on earth—I mean—I thought you went out." The woman studies her curiously. Marie forgot to take off the schoolgirl tie and part of it is peeping out above her robe. Laurent stares at her. He's ashamed for her but chooses to keep talking to dispel the embarrassment. "We're here because I forgot my file in the kitchen this morning, but we need to get back to the office soon. Oh yes, I'd like to introduce Julia, my new coworker." Julia is beautiful. She's young, slim, willowy, molded into a beige suit that clings perfectly to her figure. Her long dark hair swept up in a ponytail brings out her golden complexion and her hazel eyes. Marie stands upright, the urge to cry constricting her throat. Julia says hello, hardly dares to look her in the eye because her makeup is so obscene.

Marie thinks it best to withdraw. "Okay then, I'll let you get on with your work. I have a lot to get on with too. Lovely to meet you, Julia." As she lifts her arm to wave to her husband a stocking slips down to her ankles. Laurent closes his eyes, shamefaced. Marie instinctively pulls the stocking back up to her thigh and holds it with her hand. The pathetic absurdity of the situation reaches its height when she spots the phallus-shaped lollipop that fell out of the bag in the corridor. Luckily no one has noticed it. She snatches it up quickly and sneaks back to the bedroom. She takes off her makeup, the mascara squishing onto the damp cotton wool in great clumps. She can hear laughter at the far end of the corridor. They must be making fun of her. Yet another humiliation. She undresses and looks at her body. A hunk of dead flesh. It's not desire that's making her do all this. She must hide, conceal. And she must go pick Thomas up from the day nursery this evening. Time ticks by.

.
.
.

You need to step on the gas, Marie. This isn't good enough. Look at the chart, you're well below your targets." Her branch manager's office is the only one with an opaque closed door, a luxury that no one but Marie still values. Her work is starting not to matter to her anymore. The criticism passes her by, she doesn't even try to justify herself. The meeting was planned for the end of the day so that Marie could mull over this conversation all night, right through till the next morning. A simple tough-love management technique.

Only Hervé is still here: "I need to finish filling in these personal files for tomorrow. You'll need to be here this time." Yet another quarterly meeting. Marie won't go to it. She doesn't know how she'll react if she sees the CEO. Perhaps she'll be frightened, sad, disgusted, or, conversely, empathetic or confident in the face of the secret that binds them. Her phone rings. "You remember we're having dinner together at the Train Bleu this evening? Did you get the babysitter on the phone?" Marie takes an interest in her son only when she can free herself of her maternal responsibilities.

As she does every evening after work, she arrives at the day nursery late. Her contract with the child-care providers stipulates that she should pick up her son at seven o'clock. Today it's eight o'clock. She apologizes to the employee who's holding Thomas in her arms. The woman eyes her reproachfully. "I'm very sorry, ma'am, but maybe you should change your contract to extend Thomas's time here by one hour a day, then everyone will know where they stand. Because this is the fifth time this week you've been late..." The other mothers turn to look at her. Not with compassion but unadulterated judgment. Marie is a bad mother, she knows she is. She says she'll discuss it with her husband, settles Thomas in his buggy, and leaves. She hears the child-care worker's voice through the door: "What about his Binky?" She doesn't stop.

———

Marie doesn't really remember when she and Laurent last had dinner at the Train Bleu. Most likely shortly after their wedding. When she arrived there that time, she wondered why her husband had arranged a romantic evening in the concourse of Gare de Lyon train station. Such a noisy place, often dirty and with some unsavory characters around in the evenings. A large mirrored staircase leads all the way up to the restaurant, whose blue sign lights up the wide arcades on the floor below. And all at once the grayness of everyday life disappears in the vast neo-Baroque architecture of the place. The station's glass roof supported on large green pillars gives the restaurant an old-fashioned charm. Marie will never tire of Paris brasseries. She spots Laurent already at a table on the left-hand side of the room. He's on the phone. He gets up from his chair and whispers to his wife: "I need to take this call, it's very important, I'll be a few minutes. You order, darling. A bottle of Pouilly-Fumé and I'll have the panfried monkfish."

She knows the monkfish is a good choice but prefers to stick to her own favorite: hare à la royale. A memory surfaces in her mind. Marie used to enjoy cooking for her guests. She didn't like being caught out when friends were coming for dinner and always allowed time to set the table beautifully, spending hours trawling through home decor shops for the rare item that would make all the difference. As a wedding gift, her mother had given them a fully equipped kitchen with a complete set of utensils and several recipe books. Marie wasn't a mother back then. She thought she was doing it all for herself, perhaps partly for her husband, but mostly so that those around her noticed her capacity for delighting other people, giving them pleasure. Later, after her pregnancy, she came up with the idea of doing a big dinner, as she used to. Sophia came with a friend called Louise, a journalist for a political magazine whom she'd met at a medical symposium of her husband's on female genital mutilation. Marie had wanted to cook hare à la royale that evening, a very complicated dish, especially in the way the meat is cut up. The whole thing could fall apart at the last minute: the stuffing could spill out, the string holding the parcel together while it cooked could snap, the block of foie gras could burn if sliced too thinly. The sauce wasn't easy to make either, but luckily a good handheld mixer could achieve a sufficiently glossy effect to get a really good presentation on the plate. Game was always very stressful. Usually when she decided to embark on this sort of culinary endeavor, she started very early in the morning and went on till late in the evening, nonstop.

From the woman's first glance at her spattered apron, Marie could tell Louise belonged to the other camp: the camp of women who don't cook but who work. Marie couldn't quite make out how Louise herself experienced the evening, but the way she judged Marie's status, however surreptitiously, left Marie with an indelibly stamped anger toward women like her. Louise exhibited her erudition with broad strokes, endlessly showed off her rhetorical prowess to impress everyone present, and shot Marie the odd faux-sympathetic glance from the kitchen doorway. She eventually made up her mind to cross the threshold as if stepping into a minefield. Marie had no desire to get to know this woman with her insincere offers of help and her clichés of a Parisian political journalist: tortoiseshell reading glasses on the top of her head, a man's tweed jacket, and suede ankle boots. Back then Marie was already completely out of her depth as a mother, overweight with greasy hair however often she washed it, and hitching up her so-last-year clothes. She pretended to be relaxed all through the meal, forcing her face to soften instead of showing the disgust that this first meeting inspired in her. The terrible truths about homemakers only emerge when these women come face to face with their enemies—working women.

The huge clock hanging in the middle of the brasserie chimes nine o'clock. Marie hasn't even noticed that the bottle of white wine is already on the table. Their food is being served. When Laurent returns she's lost track of how much time has passed. "I need to go to New York next week, for about ten days, to meet my client's wife's American lawyers. I'm so sorry, I know it's bad timing but I don't have a choice. We could ask your parents to take Thomas, I'm sure they'd be happy to. It's not fun for him being at the day nursery such long hours."

Marie hasn't told Laurent about her repeated late pickup times at the nursery. She thinks this through. It's never bad news for her to spend time alone, especially without her son. She agrees to the plan as she savors her dinner, a pleasure she hasn't experienced for a long time. The sauce is wonderful, the meat tender. She knows she won't go to work while her husband's away. She'll stay at home, making the most of this free time to do nothing. The day before Laurent leaves she'll call everyone for their news so she knows they won't disturb her later.

"We need to be sure they're not going to try some ploy behind our backs. The tiniest mistake and it would all be over. We've worked so hard on this case." Marie asks Laurent whether his boss will be making the trip with him. "No, I'm going with Julia." Just the mention of her name shatters Marie's high spirits, sweeps aside the sumptuous setting and the exquisite food, and pollutes the premises as if tons of excrement were being poured over its gilded walls, running along the skirting boards and making the molding collapse. But this isn't a humiliation too far for Marie. She'd rather concentrate on any traps liable to endanger her secret. If the space closes in on her, she'll defend herself. If possibilities open up, perhaps she'll go completely crazy before finally deciding to take action.

:

Laurent has been gone two days. Marie has entrusted Thomas to her parents, who are thrilled that she wants them to look after the child. She won't go to the bank today, or tomorrow for that matter. Officially, she's sick. She goes around with a large plastic bag, dropping all the framed photographs of Thomas and Laurent into it. She'll put them back later. She knows she won't set foot outside the apartment. She's not going to work, the alarm clock is switched off, the fridge is full, her friends are busy, Laurent is far away, her parents are looking after her son, and her phone is on silent. There's nothing left for Marie to live for. The plastic bag tears under the weight. Shards of glass scatter at her feet on the wooden floor. The photos spring out of their frames. Marie gazes at them briefly from above, carelessly nudges the debris aside with her foot. She doesn't feel like vacuuming. She drops the bag in a corner of the room and ends up lying on the sofa, waiting for something to happen even though she knows perfectly well nothing will. She has to agree to do nothing, just wait for time to pass.

She hasn't been out for a week. She goes without washing more and more frequently, staying in bed in the dark for whole days. Laurent emails her every evening to ask if everything's okay. Marie has lost two or three kilos. Her body looks flaccid and white like a battery hen's. The apartment is soon reduced to a pitiful state, filthy and untidy. On her sheets a repulsive smell mingles with the sweat from her tired, bloated body. She's stopped depilating her pubic hair and her vagina is dirty, dotted with tiny white particles. By neglecting to wash, she's refusing to comply, without expending any energy at all.

After two days of isolation she started masturbating for whole afternoons at a stretch, taking her pleasure to suit herself, independent of the false reflection of gratification that a man's attention produces in a woman when she reaches orgasm. She keeps herself going as best she can with the medication she finds. She takes several sleeping pills a day to make the time pass more quickly. No more links with reality or the outside world: she has stopped charging her cell phone and her Internet connection serves only to maintain a link with Laurent. She never turns on the TV. She doesn't want to hear other people's noise. More often than not she lounges on the sofa producing slime like a snail. Her hollow face and desperate eyes are the last pleas of someone condemned to death.

Marie is sad, she's so ugly, her face and body already ruined. At just thirty-two and destroyed by a lack of life, she sometimes feels as if her blood has stopped flowing, as if it's stagnating in her exhausted limbs. She tries to survive, to keep her head above water without for a moment envisioning having enough energy to keep on getting up in the morning. Seeing her own smile in the large windows in the living room breaks her heart with self-pity and self-loathing. She must have communicated a fear of loving into her womb, into her entrails that have long since been bogged down in the bitterness that she hopes to pass on to her son. She's afraid of her body's weakness, of her mind's progressive disintegration, of her failed gestures. Everything about her betrays mediocrity, her every attempt to plow on with a dignified life reinforces her intrinsic infirmity, and yet she gets the impression she's still just about breathing. This could go on for years, but the baby is crying somewhere far away from her. He'll be coming back into her life.

Dear Laurent,

You don't know who I am or the state I'm in as I write to you now. You don't know your own wife. I watch porn films like you. Sitting on the sofa with my laptop on my knees and my panties around my ankles, I drive my fingers into my dirty, hairy pussy and bring them up to my mouth, they smell disgusting, but I really like it. I stopped washing myself and brushing my teeth. I'm not working, not talking, not tidying up, not doing the housework, not changing the sheets or my clothes, not airing the rooms, I stopped flushing the toilet, stopped depilating my pubes, stopped wearing makeup, I'm filling my face with sleeping pills, I stopped throwing my pantyliners in the trash and I have fast food delivered every day. I don't have any contact with anyone, except once, yesterday, with the checkout girl when I went down to buy some bottles of Coke. I'm not happy but I'm not unhappy either. I'm just waiting for it to be over and most of all avoiding anything energetic. I think a woman can be totally liberated when it's not her mind that makes the decisions but her body.

I was raped. You didn't notice anything. Had in every orifice from my pussy to my ass, my ass to my mouth, on the seat of a car while you ate and drank happily with your boss in a restaurant. I didn't say anything. I went to bed like a good girl, with my body burning, my vagina distended, rubbed raw, bleeding. You went right on destroying my body, ramming it with your fat cock and your fingers.

Thomas isn't your son. He's just the product of my assault. I wanted to kill him before he was born by falling down the stairs at my parents' house. I also tried to make myself miscarry in the hospital by driving a penknife into my womb but the doctor didn't give me time to do it so I gave up. I carried that child of misery for nine months. I've never been able to wash him because his penis disgusts me. I used to smother him in nice-smelling cream so you didn't notice the stench coming from his cot when you came home from work. Your first intuition was right. I did try to throw him out that night when you saw me on the balcony. I've been lying to you from the start and you didn't notice a thing, you forgive me, you keep justifying my behavior, saying I'm tired and stressed. Roxane, my parents, Sophia, or even Paul—your great gynecologist friend—never *tried to understand me. I hate Thomas. I'd like to see him lying dead in my arms someday. I want this nightmare to stop at last. I've felt trapped, humiliated, tormented. And I've made some choices. I've chosen my options as best I could, out of instinct and conscience.*

While I'm waiting for you to come back, I'm devoting a lot of time to the pleasure of doing nothing, to be sure everything is just fine. Right now, it's my pussy that decides when I should masturbate, my body that rejects or accepts personal hygiene, the only resistance to this fatalistic approach comes from what's left of my sensible mind. Lying in sheets stained with blood and sweat, I can finally make out the possibility of feeling my body quite independently of your male opinion, judgment, and will. A neighbor from the second floor came and rang the doorbell earlier. He complained about the stink in the corridor but I didn't open the door to him, because I now think throwing things in the trash is just another modern pastime we should avoid.

Marie

Marie saves the letter as "MLT"—Marie Laurent Thomas—and shuts down her computer. Everything is perfectly in order, she feels a sense of total relief. Her only thought now is that just "ML" would have been enough.

The shrill bell on the intercom rings through the apartment. It's five thirty p.m. and Marie's still in bed. She struggles to open her eyes to squint at the red numbers on her alarm clock. She remembers yesterday evening. She felt like having cocktails with vodka and pineapple juice. As she drained her third glass she realized she'd taken two sleeping pills a couple of hours earlier. The combination of alcohol and medication sent her into a deep sleep at just six in the evening. She gets up. Her head spins. She's going to throw up. The bell is still invading her home. Someone's determined to disturb her. She hasn't tidied the apartment. She traipses into the corridor, crushes an orange juice carton.

The sticky liquid spills over the floor. She kicks aside several greasy fast-food boxes, slides along a wall to reach the front door. Her husband's entire collection of miniature cars crashes to the floor. The broken pieces roll away, disappearing between the deep floorboards. Marie can't open her eyes properly, the sleeping pills are still having a powerful effect. With one last effort, resting her elbows on the console table in the hall to stay on her feet, she manages to grab the handset of the intercom. Knowing she won't be able to articulate a single word, she waits for an answer.

"Marie? It's Mom." Her mother is bringing the baby back. Marie drops the handset. Her mother yells to be let in, Marie automatically presses the button. Her body sways forward, backward, in every direction, like a lonely boat in the middle of a storm. She's lost all her bearings, lost the energy to justify herself, fight her corner, clean, tidy up. Her brain isn't getting enough blood anymore. It's too late. She wants to lie down. She heads back to the living room and brushes the leftovers of pizza onto the carpet.

She hears her mother arrive and open the door. "Marie? Where the heck are you?" Then silence. Marie wants to sleep. She can feel her mother's concern. Thomas is in his buggy, whimpering. "What the hell happened here? You...you need to get some fresh air in here. Marie! What *is* this?" Irene shakes her daughter's inert body. She surveys the room. Marie tells her she took some sleeping pills the day before and that she's still under the influence of them. Her mother gets up, draws back the curtains and opens all the windows one by one. A fresh breeze floods the apartment. There's air inside again. Irene starts tidying up: with a garbage bag in one hand she picks up the detritus strewn all over the floor. "I'm going to make you a big mug of strong coffee to wake you up." Marie hears water running. Her mother helps her to her feet, strips her completely naked. There's dried blood on her thighs. Her pubic area is dirty, her armpits give off a strong smell of sweat that pervades the whole bathroom, there are long trails of white and yellow in her panties. Irene lifts her up to help her into the scalding water. Marie's hands are filthy too, her black nails cling to her mother's skinny arms while Irene battles with all her strength to hold her upright in the bath. Marie closes her eyes, her head leaning on the edge of the tub. Her face is gaunt, pained, puffy in places like an old hobo who has spent all her winters out of doors. "You relax. I'll be back, I'm going to clean up the apartment and deal with Thomas. I'm staying here tonight."

In the kitchen, Irene gathers all the plates and things piled up in the sink and puts them into the dishwasher. She doesn't understand her daughter. She remembers Marie was always a mysterious little girl.

As a child, she never lied, but she told the truth only if asked direct questions. Marie's father also cultivates this tendency for secrecy. Irene's cell phone rings. She comes back into the living room from the kitchen that's strewn with trash. It's Laurent: "I can't get hold of Marie. I'm kind of worried. Is everything okay? Are you at the apartment with her and Thomas?" Irene says she is, reassures him, tells him everything's fine and there's no need to worry. He's coming home tomorrow evening. She'll have time to clean everything up and deal with her daughter before he's back.

She spots the pile of broken photo frames in the corner of the living room. She picks up the picture of Thomas and Laurent and puts it on the sideboard. "I forgot to put them back." Marie is standing behind her mother. Water drips heavily from the ends of her wet hair.

"You can explain tomorrow if you want to. Right now, off to bed with you or you'll fall over."

Marie drifts away, dragging her feet. She isn't ashamed. There are few women who are genuinely misanthropic and dare to shoulder the onus for not being productive and sociable. A man's sloppiness is often seen as more natural, an expression of free-spiritedness even. A woman's goes against nature. Over the course of this short week, Marie has felt rather proud that she belonged to this new generation of women who don't do a fucking thing and whose only progeny is their own pleasure. Irene works her way through the chaos left by her daughter. Thomas watches from a distance, still strapped into his buggy. Impotently witnessing the catastrophe of his birth.

Marie is rested. She goes to pick up her husband from Charles de Gaulle Airport. His flight from New York is on time and the arrivals gate opens at last. Laurent appears with Julia. They walk side by side, joking together, patting each other's shoulders. Marie feels anger build inside her. Her hands tighten on the handle of Thomas's buggy. Wrapped in his big sky-blue blanket, little Thomas is quiet. Laurent is happy to see his family and hurries over to them. He goes to his son first, then turns to his wife. Julia stands to one side. "I'll take a taxi home." Laurent offers to drive her home instead, but she politely declines. She doesn't want to get in the way of their reunion, and gives Laurent a furtive wave. As they go their separate ways, Marie feels that Julia and her husband exchanged a strange look, like the embarrassed little smile someone might direct, with lowered eyes, at a stranger in a nightclub.

In the car Laurent starts describing his trip to Marie. He says how relieved he is to be going home where he can relax with her and Thomas, and not be subjected to endless working dinners with his client. Irene stayed at the apartment last night to look after her daughter. The two women didn't talk. Marie didn't explain the state she was in, and her mother didn't dare ask her what had happened. Laurent is home at last and everything will go back to normal.

For the first time since Marie returned to work, her young coworker Mathilde's office is empty. "The poor little thing's been ill for more than a week. No one's had any news." Marie decides to message her on the cell phone number that Mathilde gave her when they first met. She feels lost without her. Every day for months now Mathilde has helped her use the new tools introduced by the bank, reach her targets, and apply the marketing techniques she learned at college. Her absence is difficult to bear this morning.

Marie's phone vibrates in her hand. Roxane again. Yesterday Marie's sister left her three messages to which she's had neither the time nor the inclination to reply. Roxane wants to know if everything's okay since Laurent came home. She's there if Marie needs her. Her final words sound like some sort of last chance: "You can call me whenever you like. I'm here for you, always. I love you." Irene must have told her the mess Marie was in when she brought Thomas back. The apartment buried under trash, Marie collapsed on the sofa, drugged on sleeping pills, her body dirty and her mind exhausted. Her family are beginning to notice the first signs. Most people think secrets can be kept more easily with passing time, but that's not true. In the early days, a liar stays alert, vigilant, attentive to the tiniest thing that might destroy the whole construction. Usually no one notices anything, but the logic of the setup is gradually established in people's minds. They reconstruct the narrative piece by piece, grasp its incoherence, and eventually assemble the rest with elements from their own imagination, elements that inevitably prove right. Marie drives these thoughts from her mind. She's not watching one of those films where the viewer has no idea from start to finish. She's the leading lady. She's the victim who knows everything. She'll never let her story be completely revealed. She doesn't deserve to lose everything now.

———

It's six o'clock and Laurent is due to pick up Thomas from the day nursery this evening. Marie makes the most of this freedom by strolling along the boulevard Magenta. Rain spatters onto her coat. She forgot her umbrella at the office, a major mistake for anyone who lives in Paris. The little stores are still open. She'd like to buy a good steak for Laurent. She'll serve it with a pepper sauce and roasted potatoes. She's about to go into the butcher's shop when she suddenly notices some tables outside a bistro on a street corner across the avenue. "If you're not coming in, shut the door!" The butcher's powerful voice startles Marie and she slams the door noisily, to the astonishment of all the customers.

She goes over to one of the bistro tables. Lit up by the infrared heating element on the terrace is Mathilde, Marie's young coworker, slumped in a chair. She's unrecognizable. Her eyes stare vacantly. Marie is standing in front of her, only a few yards from her table, but Mathilde hasn't noticed her. She downs her glass in one swallow. Judging from her state, Marie guesses the drink must be strong liquor. The clothes Mathilde is wearing are the same as she wears to work but they're badly crumpled and have stains on them. Her hair, soaked from the rain, has been pulled carelessly into a topknot. She clutches clumsily at a passing waiter to ask him for another whiskey and Coke. He tells her she should maybe think about stopping. She retorts that he should go fuck himself. Marie steps slowly closer and says her name quietly. Mathilde doesn't seem to recognize her. Marie sits at the next table to talk to her. She asks her what's going on, whether she can help her, why she's stopped coming to work. Mathilde ignores her for several minutes, rambles aimlessly, calls her a "hopeless case" because of her kid, and sets off on meaningless alcohol-fueled rants. Marie would like to help her but decides she must give up. Now's not the time. She's about to leave when Mathilde grabs her by the sleeve of her coat. Her face lights up at last, then tenses. Tears spill over her cheeks, streaking them. She sobs, her hands shake. "Why do men do that to women? I didn't do anything, didn't ask for anything! I was happy at the bank, you know...With you I could make myself useful...and...I'd rather die than go back there. Never again!" Marie freezes. Her limbs stiffen. She can't stay sitting, her vagina hurts. She's ricocheted back to that night all over again. The sky was the same, dark and damp. Did he take advantage of her in the car too? Was she subjected to the same torments? How long did her rape go on? Did he come inside her? All these questions remain unspoken. No advice, no guidance can be offered. Marie is overpowered by, broken by her responsibility. This poor child was raped by the same man and almost certainly in the same way as she herself was. Mathilde lets go of Marie's coat and sips at the dregs in her glass. Marie goes up to the bar to pay Mathilde's bill. She lifts the young woman's slender body and supports her under her shoulder to reach the taxi stand opposite the bistro. The girl isn't heavy. He can't have found it difficult getting the better of her. Child's play for a man of his strength.

Mathilde falls asleep in the taxi. When they arrive outside her building, Marie helps her out and goes to the door with her to be sure she gets into her apartment safely. Mathilde lives in a small studio of about thirty-five square meters. The exotic decor suits her: vibrant, young, exciting, full of life. Marie looks at her exhausted, damaged body as she lies down on the sofa, her stained jeans and her dirty hair straggling over the orange cushions. Mathilde doesn't seem to belong in her studio at all now. Nothing makes sense anymore.

Marie slips away, closes the door softly, and goes back out to the taxi to go home. It's her fault. If she'd reported the rape the CEO wouldn't have found another victim. Mathilde's traumatized expression in the red glow on the terrace, her features strained with anguish, her breath reeking of liquor—it could all have been avoided if she, Marie, hadn't been such a coward. She'll never forgive herself. She feels as if she's suffocating in the taxi. She arches her body, can't bear the rain relentlessly striking the windshield and the repeated military-sounding noise of the windshield wipers, like sharp thrusts of the hips. "Stop! Let me out here, I want to walk." The driver refuses, protesting that they're half way down a wide avenue and there's nowhere to pull over. Marie opens the door with the car still moving. The driver slams on his brakes. Marie throws a twenty-euro note onto the dashboard and alights in the bustle of the avenue de l'Opéra, to the driver's receding yells. The fresh air and driving rain whip her face, awakening her energy. The facade of the Opéra Garnier lights up both sides of the avenue. The entrance to the Métro station is teeming with a dense crowd of people, swallowing and spitting back out thousands of travelers over the course of a day, the old subterranean walls constricting, suffering for want of air. Marie wanders aimlessly, she's jostled, pushed, knocked over, and elbowed several times. She wants people to hurt her, wants them to make her pay for her silence. Her torture isn't cruel enough, the price she's paying is too low.

Back at home, Marie stands in the corridor watching the heartwarming sight of her husband and son playing together on the carpet. She takes off her coat and comes over to Laurent, smiling. He turns around: "You finished late today... but don't worry, I made you some dinner. It's duck breast and dauphinois potatoes this evening." There's a fake, toxic happiness to it all, like something from a fascist propaganda poster about the miraculous joy afforded by time spent with loved ones. And this fakery so readily disguises unhappiness.

When they've eaten, Laurent puts Thomas to bed in his room. As she does every evening, Marie pretends to kiss her son good night before he goes to sleep. She stays leaning over the cot, stares at the child for a while, listens to him whimper as he reaches up his little arms helplessly, then she turns away without a word and goes to join her husband in the living room.

Laurent has put two glasses of Marie's favorite drink—white wine with black currant liqueur—on the coffee table. He wants to tell her how much he loves her and how grateful he is for everything that she does from day to day for the sake of their family. Marie smiles. She knows. He's going to touch her again. The signal has been given, just like every time he suggests a drink after dinner. She understands that her husband is frustrated. He doesn't want to cheat on her by having an affair with his coworker Julia. Too complicated, too risky when they've just had their first child. So he compensates by touching Marie's ass and breasts and pussy. She feels herself fingered, fumbled, lets him have his way as usual. She thinks of Mathilde, of how she was raped by the CEO. He must have used the same process of intimidation, the same moves. Laurent's hands are prying gently inside her panties. His penis stiffens, seeking out its route, sniffing the smell of her moist cavities like a dog. Young Mathilde will become an alcoholic. Laurent pushes her onto the sofa, stuffs his fingers into her mouth, pins her down lightly by the shoulders. Mathilde is only twenty-two. He penetrates her, thrusts powerfully deep inside her. He moans. She thinks. Her thighs rub against the fabric, chafing her skin. Mathilde is lost. He withdraws from her, directs his penis toward her mouth. She could have told Mathilde about her experience. The to-and-fro of his shaft in her mouth accelerates. She sucks, presses, swallows, covers the tip of his swollen glans with little licks, gathers saliva and precum in the same place. He doesn't want to come yet, holds back so he can keep going. With long deliberate movements he licks her wet pussy, getting the long pubic hairs that she refuses to shave in his mouth and drawing them out with his fingers. Mathilde absolutely must take the morning-after pill so she doesn't get pregnant. She rubs his penis hard, violently, burying her face in the crook of his neck so that he doesn't see her, so that he finally stops fucking her. She could help her with what she needs to do, be her friend, her confidante, her guide. A long cry of relief and he discharges, empties himself onto her, just the way he likes to. The viscous white fluid spreads over

Marie's breasts, trickles onto her stomach like the last spurt of a blocked tube. Laurent relaxes. Marie starts breathing again, she holds her breath every time her husband touches her. She stays still while he puffs and pants reaching the pleasure he always achieves.

Women are just a hole. A huge vacuum of soft flesh. A guilty moist desert, and right in the middle of it the man plies his way, like a god.

The child-care worker eyes her suspiciously. But Marie is in fact on time for once. She finishes strapping Thomas into his buggy and leaves to the whispering of other mothers. Laurent is completely absorbed by his work and has virtually no time to help her. He comes home late at night, leaves early in the morning, and brings files home on the weekend. Marie thinks he must be spending more time with Julia than with his family. Thomas is crying in his buggy. He lost his Binky along the way. Everyone in the street turns to look as they pass, wondering what sort of mother lets her child scream without doing a thing. Marie hands him her cell phone to play with so that he'll shut up at last. The baby toys with the luminous object, fascinated, but after a few seconds he throws it to the ground. It shatters into several parts on the concrete. Intense anger spreads through Marie's stomach. She picks up the plastic pieces and puts them in her bag. She lowers herself till she's on a level with her son and takes hold of him gently so no one will notice. Her nails dig into the fleecy blanket that's always wrapped around Thomas. She squeezes his hands till his face contorts in pain. Still crouching in front of the buggy with her head leaning inside it, she brings her hands up to his neck to squeeze even tighter. She's going to strangle him now. No passerby could notice a baby killed by strangulation in his buggy, they'll think he's sound asleep. Thomas gasps, struggles helplessly, waving his little hands. With one hand his mother squeezes his throat tighter. His eyes are starting to go red with the early effects of asphyxia. Marie doesn't stop. The child's chubby neck burrows deep into the cushion. His feet pummel the buggy's footrest. Marie puts a finger down his throat and he immediately throws up.

Marie gradually releases her hold. Thomas breathes, coughs, has trouble swallowing. She can't, not like this. It's too difficult. Her blouse is soaked with sweat and tears. She collapses, falls apart right there in front of her son who now seems to be smiling at her again. No one walks past. She looks at her child. He's happy to be alive. Only his mother wants him gone. She hauls herself to her feet, her every move heavy, awkward, requiring a great effort of will. She brushes down her coat quickly with the back of her hand and dead leaves flitter away. She watches them all the way up into the sky. Her head tips back, she loses her balance, her feet are no longer on the ground. She can't go on, her legs keep giving way under the pressure and the sadness. She manages to get over to a bench. One of those green benches with slats of dry wood that split and catch on clothing. One of those ubiquitous Parisian seats that no one notices anymore. There's one opposite Marie's apartment. Every morning she watches a woman who sits alone, crossed-legged on that bench. And then, at about eight thirty, she gets up and leaves. Now Marie's the one consoling her loneliness on a public bench. It's genuinely miserable, allows you to gauge just how powerless you are. Her reality has been completely destroyed, crushed, prostrated by sadness. Everything is beyond her and she has nothing to cling to. The shadow of a man looms before her, dark and imposing, frightening. Man in general, the male sex. Her bottom lip bleeds onto her white blouse. Thomas scratched her during the struggle, he defended himself to stop his mother going all the way. There are children playing in a small square nearby. And at this moment, here in this nonsilence interrupted by laughter and crying, Marie understands what she has set in motion. From where she's sitting on the bench, she turns to look at her son and, her face overwhelmed with distress, she grants him a few moments' peace. "I'm so sorry."

Thomas is asleep in his room, far from danger, sheltered from his mother. Marie has watched very little television in the last several years, she's hardly listened to the radio and read very few newspapers, except perhaps when she feels sorry for those people who stand outside the Métro station in the rain handing out great piles of free papers. She is totally isolated from current affairs. She just listens to her clients telling her the latest news of this ailing world. They're careful to mention only the bad news, no one ever wants to put her in a good mood.

Lying on the sofa in the living room, leaning against her small woolen cushion, she flicks through a magazine and casts an eye at the TV news headlines. Her husband's face appears on-screen. Marie jumps up, throws herself onto the floor to grab the remote. She turns up the volume. Laurent is on the steps of the Paris law courts surrounded by about fifty TV cameras. Hounded up against one of the building's large columns, his arms laden with different-colored files, he appears measured, confident, and unruffled as he answers journalists' questions. He always tells his wife that to be a good lawyer the main thing is to think of justice as a huge theater in which everyone is playing a part. He must always play the same one: the conqueror.

"In this divorce case, which is essentially about a fair distribution of Monsieur Ponce's assets, my client does not have to answer to the additional accusations that have been disseminated in the media over the last few days for purely provocative purposes and, furthermore, that are totally unfounded. It's strange that these accusations have only emerged now, and some people would want them to be upheld to benefit Madame Ponce." Laurent does not use the word "rape" or even "assault." Marie stays at the foot of the sofa to watch. The piece finishes abruptly after her husband's contribution, and is followed by another item about the disturbing rise in autumnal temperatures this year. She goes to the kitchen to pour herself a glass of wine. She leans on the counter for a long time, thinking about how Laurent is also hiding the facts and about how the women at the day nursery and even some of her clients judged her today.

Half an hour later she hears her husband come home. He's exhausted. Breathing heavily, he hangs his coat in the hall, laboriously takes off his shoes, and then stops for a moment. Standing motionless in the corridor he fires himself up again like a worn-out machine, and goes to join Marie in the kitchen. "I'm dead beat. Today went on forever...Journalists really are a pain in the neck, like a swarm of flies. They won't give up!" He grabs the bottle of wine from the countertop, takes a glass from the sink, and fills it to the brim.

Marie watches him steadily. "But is it true?"

Laurent puts down his glass and frowns as if her question is as stupid as it's incomprehensible. He doesn't understand.

"Did he really rape that girl? This friend of his daughter's? Did he assault her?" Silence, again and as usual. Laurent looks away, tells his wife he's tired, that he'd like to come home to some peace and not be hounded by more questions. He's getting angry. Marie remains stoic in the face of his fury, asks the same question again several times. Laurent is exasperated, he explodes, flushes red. He doesn't understand why she's so insistent. Marie tells him that she's humiliated, that everyone's judging her because her husband's defending a rapist; she can feel it at the nursery and at the bank, and she wants a definitive, honest answer.

"Do you really want to know? Yes, he did it. He raped the girl when she came to his place for a vacation with his daughter. Are you happy? Satisfied?"

Marie is petrified by Laurent's answer. He knows he went too far. He's at the end of his rope too. He drops his voice: "He admitted it to me yesterday evening. I haven't spoken with the lawyer who's dealing with that yet. But you do understand I'm just defending him for his divorce case, not for accusations of rape. I shouldn't even be talking to you about it, I'm bound by professional confidentiality. But I don't know, this case seems to mean so much to you that..."

Marie is still like a slab of marble. She interrupts him and asks him coldly to repeat what his client admitted.

Laurent is uncomfortable but agrees to reveal a few details: "Well, he told me he was a little drunk that afternoon. That the girl had been giving him the eye right from the start of the vacation. And then...he doesn't really know how...Well, he lost control and he had sexual relations with her. He told me that at first she consented, but she started struggling after a few minutes." Laurent stops talking. Marie waits to hear more, staring at him, holding her breath, suffocating. "He just couldn't stop...He forced her and ended up raping her. Several times."

Laurent is ashamed, he lowers his head. Marie's eyes fill with tears. Her husband puts a hand on her arm. She pushes him back violently against the counter. A glass breaks. Shards fly in every direction. He apologizes. He wasn't aware of his client's actions before he accepted the divorce case, or he would never have taken him on. He's stuck now. Marie tries to contain her hysteria but it's just too strong. She picks up the porcelain vase on the windowsill and flings it at her husband, who ducks to avoid it. She hurls insults at him, calls him a bastard, a savage primitive prick, defending a child rapist, the devil's own lawyer. She can't stop herself now, throwing anything she can get her hands on at his face. He dodges and ducks and eventually throws himself on top of her to restrain her. He yells at her, asks her to calm down, squeezes her arms, rams his thighs against hers to keep her on the floor. His shouting intensifies. Marie fights with all her strength, spits in his face, tries to knee him in the groin. In the end he slaps her violently. Terrified by what he's done, he relaxes his hold on his wife's body. He backs away in silence, apologizes. He should never have hit her. It's the first time. The madness of it is raw. Marie is still on the floor. Thomas has woken, his wails reverberating in the corridor. The baby monitor vibrates on the dining table. Marie sighs: "Go deal with your son, honey. Seeing as you're so fond of rapists."

Marie's psychotic expression and her little smile terrify Laurent. Whatever the circumstances, even in future moments of happiness, he'll never be able to forget that smile. The slap, his wife's battered face as she lies on the floor, and those enigmatic words that he doesn't even have the courage to ask her to explain for fear of triggering more anger. Tough, he'll have to live with the doubt. He gets up, wipes Marie's spit from the corners of his mouth with his sleeve, and goes off to see his son. She knows the end is near. She couldn't say exactly how she can tell but something has changed this evening.

⋮

This Tuesday morning Mathilde came back to work. Nearly three months after she left. Marie hasn't called her and hasn't tried to get any news of her since she came across her at that bar on the boulevard Magenta. She's afraid to see her again. Her not very empathetic reaction to the girl's rape must have aroused some suspicions in her. Marie is careful not to meet her over the course of the day. She knows she'll have to work with her on their shared files but would rather Mathilde came to her.

Marie can no longer bear to feel her cell vibrate in her pocket. It's the fifth time in two days that Roxane has called to see how she is. She always asks the same questions, asks whether everything's okay, how little

Thomas is doing, whether Laurent's highly publicized case is going well. But she refuses to talk about what happened with their mother. "I'm not judging you. People do just get depressed sometimes." It's not depression. Marie, just like Mathilde, isn't depressive. They haven't fallen into drug use, alcoholism, or prostitution. They haven't left Paris or the bank for which their rapist still works. They've just carried on living without talking about it, hiding their misery in the comforting routines of their tidy, privileged, day-to-day lives. It's the framework within which they circulate that causes their downfall.

Marie is cooped up in what people generally call a "happy marriage." It's what she'd always hoped for: a genuine love match with a man she cherished and admired. Laurent was that man and is now her husband. And she wanted children too. Thomas came along. Should she regret the fact that she wanted to preserve a happiness that not many people ever experience, simply for the sake of honesty? She would have ruined three lives.

In Mathilde's case, the effect on her relationship is a little different. She had confided in Marie that she'd had a boyfriend for a few months but in the meantime had met another student at college and had fallen in love with him straightaway. She's planning to leave her boyfriend and start a new relationship. She takes, loves, dumps. Then starts again, loves all over again, dumps all over again. Girls of Mathilde's generation often find themselves stuck between two very different concepts of loving relationships. On the one hand they can make the most of sexual relations outside married life, changing partners whenever an interesting opportunity arises and enjoying their freedom. But this availability can also give rise to a longing for the opposite: to protect themselves from a freedom that ends up being frightening or abusive. Some devote their efforts to finding the one love, coveting the enduring performance of a successful marriage and faithfulness. It's rather reminiscent of the banking packages that Marie sometimes sells to her clients. Depending on the formula, they are sent a bank card, a checkbook, insurance, and occasionally even a teddy bear to mark the beginning of a wonderful, strong relationship with the bank. Mathilde has admitted to her that she'd like to get married and have children one day. Perhaps she already has one growing inside her?

The bank is closed. It's perfectly silent. Some of the lights are out. Everything has lost its shiny brightness. The room where the printers are is always lit up by harsh neon tubes. Marie often has a migraine for the rest of the day after being in here. Today she's printing out contracts that need signing for her meetings tomorrow, and she won't finish till about six thirty. As she concentrates on the printer-copier, she becomes aware of a presence behind her. Her heart tears her chest in two. She can hear breathing, notices the shadow growing in the doorway, sliding over the white walls. Marie keeps taking out the pages and piling them on one side of the bulky machine, pretends to sort through them to play for time. Her hands are shaking. A loud noise paralyzes the air. A thick ream of paper has fallen to the floor. Without moving her head, she glances down to the right and starts looking for something sharp or heavy. There's nothing obvious. She thinks her heart might give out, her breathing might stop, fear might overwhelm her. The dark shadow comes closer to the printer. A hand picks up the paper to put it back on the shelf. It's a woman's hand. Marie turns around.

"Sorry, I'm waiting for the photocopier, the other one's out of order." Ashen, Marie nods and mutters a few unintelligible words. Mathilde comes up to her, puts her hand on her shoulder, asks if she's okay. Marie turns to look at her. Their faces are close together. Their eyes bore right into each other. She can feel Mathilde's exhalations on her cheek, smell her fruity breath, a waft of her perfume. That generous, delicate floral fragrance, a combination of grapefruit and camellias with notes of vanilla, that pervades the whole bank. Marie is turned to stone, her hand still reaching toward the printer that whirs on and on. She tries to pull herself together, like someone dragging themselves out of a nightmare.

"I...I think I was scared. I was scared it wasn't you." Mathilde doesn't take her eyes off Marie. She moves closer, puts her hand slowly on the back of her neck. She's sweating. Her eyes are shining. A mist clouds Marie's eyes. Mathilde rests her head against her neck and whispers reassuringly, "It's just me." Marie closes her eyes, feels Mathilde's head pull back and turn. Her smell moves away, fading on the air. Mathilde's lips press gently onto hers. Marie submits, kisses her, puts her arms around her waist, holds her close. There's a stirring between her legs. This feels gentle, safe, understanding. Every movement is a caress, a precious moment that her body accepts. She's no longer a woman's body. She's *the* body. She is the man and the woman. She is ageless, genderless, free of guilt, anger, and suffering. It all comes to an end here, between two women. Marie is reminded of her desires from years ago. Before going to bed in the evening, in the privacy of her own room, she had fondled herself. Her panties wet, her pussy swollen and strong-smelling. At fourteen she discovered the first spasms of pleasure, when her body alone called to her. No external presence entered her intimacy. Marie alone could do anything.

When Marie opens her eyes Mathilde peels slowly away from her body, with her hands still in her hair.

They won't go any further. This kiss is a promise. Mathilde wants Marie to say nothing, just as she's learned to. Marie promises to comply. Mathilde leaves the room with one last glance at her. They study each other for a moment, seeking each other out. This isn't some old woman met by chance in the street. This is a young girl of twenty-two who was raped by and may also be pregnant by her attacker. The secret is still safe. Silence rules, forever. The two women have found each other and bow to its sovereignty. This won't be mentioned again.

．
．
．

Relations between Marie and Laurent haven't improved since their fight. The divorce case Laurent has been handling for months is about to come to an end and, according to the media, his client has every chance of salvaging three-quarters of his fortune despite the charges brought against him for raping a minor. There's no justice. Not sexually or socially. But over the last few weeks, Marie has done a lot of thinking. She regrets being irresponsible. She wants to improve the situation, repair the damage done by her fits of anger, explain to her husband just how out of proportion her reactions have been, apologize for all the times when he was totally baffled, for the strain and the fury. She forgives him for slapping her. She forgives him the trial so long as everything goes back to what it was like before.

At the end of her day's work she calls Laurent at his office to suggest they have dinner together that evening at his favorite restaurant on the Île de la Cité. He seems surprised and doesn't understand this turnaround but decides to accept. He'd like to smooth things out too. Roxane can take Thomas, to give Marie and Laurent some time alone together. Given how long Marie's sister has wanted to make herself useful, she's delighted to agree.

Marie has managed to lose two kilos this month and for her reconciliation dinner with her husband she's bought an indecently expensive black dress from Galeries Lafayette. When she tried it on a second time at home she didn't dare snip off the price tag for fear that she would realize it didn't suit her after all. Laurent is getting ready in the bathroom. She likes watching him get dressed and brush his hair, likes the smell of deodorant, the brusque regular sound of his razor on his skin, and then the quiver of the water in the basin. She sometimes thinks this intimacy should be enough for her to admit everything to him straightaway, not to wait any longer. She could tell him all of it, explain her situation from the start, the terrible chain of events in which she's been trapped. Months of instability, lies, and desperate attempts to end it all. But she can't find the courage. She holds her tongue and helps Laurent tie his tie. He looks at her affectionately. He feels as if he's never loved his wife as much as he does this evening. "You look fantastic, darling. I love you, you know how much I love you." He puts his arms around her, kisses her, breathes in the smell of her. Marie stands stiffly upright but eventually relaxes, afraid of ruining this first conciliatory move in her evening with her husband.

Roxane arrives laden with toys, candy, and packets of potato chips. Laurent and Marie greet her side by side in the corridor. "You two look stunning! I'm not in the same league in my sweatpants, but I'm going to have a great evening too with my gorgeous little nephew." Roxane goes over to Thomas and picks him up. She cuddles him, presses her face up to his, and plants soft kisses on his forehead, hands, and feet. Thomas smiles. The taxi has arrived; Laurent and Marie say one last goodbye to their son and Roxane, then leave the apartment.

It's the first time since they moved here that Laurent takes his wife's hand as they go downstairs. She feels twenty years old. She's flooded with memories. The way Laurent looks at her has the same destabilizing effect as it did when they first met at that student party. Sometimes time flies by so quickly. Then the days got longer and longer as if the clock had stopped working. And now she's wrinkled, worn, and man-handled, her face ravaged by invisible ordeals. But she's pleased with her reflection in the taxi window this evening: her floaty blond hair loose about her shoulders, her beautiful low-cut black dress, and her made-up eyes. She recognizes her old self. Laurent meanwhile never changes. He grows better-looking with each passing day, even more so this evening. The Île de la Cité comes into view. At night, Paris cradles it, allowing its beauty to dazzle. The waters of the Seine reflect every detail of the buildings along its banks. Notre-Dame cathedral keeps watch from a distance, protecting the surrounding neighborhoods. What Laurent really loves is strolling around this area and having ice cream at Bertillon in August when the heat pervades the law courts.

The restaurant is full but not too noisy. People know how to behave. The maître d' shows them to their table. Marie looks out at the barges moored along the Seine. She could stay here for hours, immersed in this Parisian cityscape she so loves. All the lights and the beauty of it touch her right to the heart. Her throat tightens. She looks at her husband; she's going to tell him everything. He loves her. She can't go on lying to him like this. Laurent takes her hand, he's feeling emotional too. Their waiter interrupts this little moment to take their order. "We've chosen the tasting menu. And a bottle of Veuve Clicquot brut, my wife's favorite."

Marie smiles. But she can't help thinking about Laurent's client. It's a child rapist who's paying for this meal, thanks to the exorbitant fees her husband is getting. She pushes the thought aside. Mathilde's kiss pops into her head. Everything is merging together. She struggles, grimaces, smiles. Laurent doesn't notice anything and they continue with their dinner.

Roxane sits on the sofa rocking Thomas, then gets up to put him down in his room. He falls asleep immediately, but she still feels happier taking the baby monitor into the living room. She's planning to watch a film this evening, but she can't choose one. When she asks her husband's advice she's always disappointed by his recommendations, which tend to be American blockbusters. Never mind, if she types "must-see films" into a search engine she's bound to find something interesting to download. She looks around the room for her sister's computer. It's not in the living room so she goes into Marie's bedroom. The laptop is closed, sitting in plain sight on her desk near the window. She takes it back into the living room and opens it. The screen lights up. She needs to put in a password. Marie once admitted to her that she uses the same password for everything on her computer: her name, then her sister's and her mother's followed by the year of her birth, with no spaces—MarieRoxaneIrene80. Roxane thought this mnemonic method very dubious in view of the hacking risks but didn't want to tell Marie for fear of panicking her. A dozen windows open up in different programs, and she closes them one by one. "Dear Laurent, You don't know who I am or the state I'm in..." Roxane can't help reading on. The words lead from one to the next, she doesn't stop. The violence of it builds. Her eyes hurt from reading quickly. Her heart breaks, her chest is about to explode. She slams the laptop shut. She can't take any more. She understands perfectly. She sits there sobbing, suddenly having trouble catching her breath, paralyzed by her distress. She's suffocating. She decides to throw open a window, and a man waves to her from the building opposite. Roxane looks at him with disgust. The computer is still on the sofa. She goes back to it to reread Marie's letter. It delivers the same shock all over again. Her sister didn't write this letter. The words are too strong, too brutal, terrifyingly dangerous, dirty. This letter's just a bundle of filth, written by a madwoman in heat. Killing her child, lying to her husband and family, trying to kill herself. No circumstances could justify that, not even rape. The baby's innocent. So much energy expended on such heinous, murderous decisions can't stay secret any longer. She needs to talk to her sister. Marie must tell Laurent the truth or she will herself.

Their dessert is served: Granny Smith apples, almond éclair, and lemon meringue pie. It's all perfect, the meal opulent, the setting sublime. Laurent brushes his legs against Marie's under the table. Everything's back to normal for the space of an evening. "It's such a long time since we had an evening this good together. Do you know there was a time when I thought I was going to lose you, I thought my wife had disappeared." Now's the time. She's going to tell him. He wouldn't dare make a scene in such a lovely place. He'll feel terrible for his wife, may even be compassionate. "But that's over now. Everything's like before, nothing's changed. I'm still just as crazy about you, Marie." She can't, it's too difficult.

Laurent doesn't give her a chance to tell the truth. He decides it's time to go and pays the check. Marie asks at reception if someone could call a taxi for them, but Laurent says no, he'd like to make the most of this wonderful evening to walk along the banks of the Seine with his wife. The evening must never come to an end. The receptionist is touched by the couple's genuine, straightforward, grown-up kind of love. Marie accepts his suggestion and puts on her coat. It's a mild night, they'll go for a stroll. In search of lost pleasure, love reconstitutes itself.

Roxane has been searching for hours for some secondary proof: a letter, a clue, a photograph, an email, something hidden or deleted from her sister's Internet search history. Nothing. Just the letter. She doesn't know what to do when the couple comes home. Should she pretend to be normal or reveal everything straight out in front of Laurent? She yo-yos between a state of panic and moments of clear reasoning. With her cell phone clutched in her hand, she wants to call her mother to tell her everything. In the end she thinks that's a terrible idea. Better to wait awhile. She sits down to think it over, then jumps up and goes to Thomas's room. He's sound asleep. His musical mobile projects hundreds of bright stars on the walls of the room. Standing on tiptoe, Roxane leans silently over Thomas's bed. She's looking for something, scrutinizing every inch of the child. From his nose to his hands, the shape of his eyes to the tips of his toes. She sees absolutely no resemblance. Roxane feels ashamed, ashamed of herself and of what she's doing. It doesn't matter if Laurent isn't the baby's father, she loves her nephew. She'll always love him. She decides to go back to the living room. It's gone midnight, Marie and Laurent will be home soon. She's cold and can smell the damp sweat of fear permeating her clothes. Her clammy hands don't seem to work properly, her body's detaching itself from her mind. Her cell phone pings: a message from Marie saying they'll be home in about an hour. She won't last that long, she can feel she's getting sick. She feels nauseous and runs to the bathroom to throw up her potato chips and cheese. Too late. Slimy yellow and red chunks spatter onto the wooden floor in the corridor. She collapses against the wall, tears spilling down her cheeks. She gets up and goes to the kitchen for a plastic bag, scoops up the half-digested food and puts it in the bag. There's a strong acidic smell. She remembers what her mother told her just after she came away from Marie's apartment, the day after she dropped off Thomas: "I even found vomit and pantyliners full of blood on the floor in the kitchen."

It's two a.m. and Roxane has fallen asleep. Marie wakes her gently. "You can stay the night here, sweetheart, but don't stay on the floor, I'll make up the sofa bed." Roxane opens her eyes and suddenly sees her sister's face. She's startled and jumps to her feet. Marie's surprised, wonders what's going on. Roxane talks loudly, panicking, looking around for her bag and coat. "No, I have to go. I—I need to—I have a lot to do in the morning. I really, I need to go." Laurent catches up with her in the corridor and asks her at least to wait until he's called a taxi. Roxane refuses, says she'll find one on the street. She's so overwhelmed and disoriented that she doesn't know how to behave toward Marie, she doesn't even take the time to put on her coat, snatches her scarf so savagely from its hook that the thing pulls out of the wall, then she races off down the stairs.

The closed laptop is still on the carpet. Marie looks down and notices it there. A beat. She thought she left it in the bedroom. She looks up again and runs off to catch up with her sister. She tells her to call to let her know she's home safely, as usual. Roxane ignores her and keeps running down the stairs.

Laurent and Marie are drunk. They've had a bottle of champagne, a liter of wine, and several digestifs. They're not aware of what has gone on. Life and liquor give them a little more respite before the catastrophe. Laurent collapses onto the sofa and Marie lies down on top of him. They fall asleep cuddled together, peaceful and trusting.

：

Marie's nerves are sorely tested this morning: the bank is seething with clients. Through her glass door she can see the line waiting behind the counter. She and Laurent did a whole year's worth of drinking last night. She doesn't clearly remember arriving home, it's all muddled, but she remembers her sister's strange behavior. Roxane absolutely refused to stay the night, claiming she had important things to do in the morning. She ran off down the stairs without calling a taxi and without letting Marie know whether she got home safely. Marie picks up her glass of soluble aspirin and drinks it down in one. Then she picks up her phone to call her sister. It goes straight to voicemail. It's only nine o'clock, maybe she hasn't had a chance to turn her phone on this morning. Marie calls her mother, who doesn't answer either. Feeling slightly light-headed, Marie decides to text Julien to check if everything's okay.

There's an endless succession of meetings. Mathilde hardly ever comes into her office now. Marie would like to see her, to feel her close by; she's suggested having lunch together several times but Mathilde has declined by email. She's been snowed under with work since her time off so Marie doesn't persist and spends most of her time with Hervé. Between two of her meetings he pops into her office to let her know he's leaving early today. Marie is surprised: in five years Hervé has never left before seven p.m. "It's my wife. She wants us to go out for a meal this evening." Marie pulls a face, asks whether he's sure it's not another of the Machiavellian plans his wife and daughter are so good at. "I took Cissy's cage to my neighbor this morning before coming to work. To be sure. After twenty years of marriage, I know what she's like, that Corinne."

It's one o'clock and the bank's metal shutters are closing for the staff to have their lunch. Through the muted clanking of the mechanism, Marie hears her sister's voice. She's sure of it, it's definitely her. She comes out of her office and heads for the central counter. "Do you have time for lunch, Marie?" Roxane looks very tired, her eyelids are drooping.

Marie knows her sister and knows something's wrong. "What happened to you? Why did you run off like that last night? And you didn't even text me to let me know you got home okay. You know that's the rule." Roxane doesn't answer. She seems to be looking around for something. Marie is irritated and asks her once and for all to tell her what's wrong.

In the end the two sisters decide to go out for lunch so they can talk. Marie always has a table reserved at lunchtime at the Merlot, a small brasserie on the corner of rue de Bretagne and rue des Archives. The table at the back, the same one she's had for ten years. Jonathan, her ex-boyfriend from high school, took over the restaurant about five years before she started working at the bank. Roxane hasn't uttered a word on the way to the Merlot. When walking through Paris it's never a big deal not to have a conversation; the city takes care of that itself. Passersby yelling on the phone, drivers sounding their horns, shopkeepers talking to their customers, café terraces heaving with people at the slightest ray of sunshine, and the sound of footsteps, a collective bustle on concrete. No one is ever alone in Paris.

Marie doesn't dare put pressure on her sister and waits patiently for her to open the conversation. Roxane keeps her eyes lowered, toying with a few pieces of meat on her plate. Marie calls the waiter and asks for some more mustard for her steak. She feels a strong pressure on her arm and turns back around. Roxane is now looking her right in the eye, leaning slightly toward her.

"I know everything, Marie. I read the letter on your laptop last night."

Marie stays silent. She instinctively defends herself by attacking, asking what letter she means.

"I wanted to use your computer to look for a film. The document called MLT. The one that explains clearly that Thomas isn't Laurent's son but...Well, I read the whole thing. I know what happened to you. You need to tell Laurent everything, you have no right to do this to him."

Marie stares at her for a moment. Roxane's last sentence strikes a chord. A powerful echo that she can't possibly ignore. An indescribable anger floods through her, she even pictures harming her sister: she'd like to strangle her to keep her quiet or drive a knife into her chest. Or simply rewind and erase the document. She hasn't had the heart to do that, the letter is the only proof that any of it really happened. She couldn't make up her mind to delete it. She so clearly remembers writing those words, and the physical and psychological distress she was in. Alone at home. Out of her mind and filthy. Wallowing in her own blood and shit. Roxane would never understand. Her mother betrayed her.

It doesn't matter if it was out of concern, right now her own family is turning against her.

"You know nothing, nothing about what happened. Please, please don't say anything. I don't want to tell him now, it would be too much for him. I can't do it." Roxane insists, exhausts every argument to persuade Marie to tell the truth. She keeps on talking, and all these words exasperate Marie. The compassion in Roxane's eyes disgusts her. She needs to shut up now. Roxane tells her she doesn't have a choice, she must admit to everything. She finally pronounces the word "rape" and Marie feels like slamming her plate in her face. So that the wine sauce dribbles over her exhausted features. And the food goes up her nostrils and suffocates her. She'd fall to the floor and stop talking at last. Marie grasps her sister's wrist. She squeezes it hard, crushing her forearm. She wants to break her bones. Marie slowly stands up but doesn't want to make a scene in the restaurant. Her face is very close to her sister's, her hand twisting her wrist. Roxane makes a few whimpering sounds, her eyes filled with terror. Still gripping hold of her sister, Marie finally makes up her mind to do something and in a quiet but firm voice says: "You listen to me now. Laurent's not going to know a thing because you're not going to tell him a thing. This is my business. It was my rape. Right from the start I've dealt with it just the way I wanted to. I don't need any morality lectures from a little bitch like you. I'm not the person I was. Nice little Marie who bakes orange cakes in her beautiful apartment with her nice little husband and her nice little life. I could do anything, you know. None of you know about this, none of you know anything."

Roxane is frightened of her sister for the first time. Her voice has changed, her intonations, the way she moves and the words she uses too. Marie is right: she's not the same person. Roxane snatches her wrist free. Marie sits back down slowly and asks for the check. It was a threat, just a threat. Clear and eloquent. Roxane takes her coat from the back of her chair and leaves the restaurant without a word. Marie reels from the shock of the confrontation. She's never talked like that to anyone. Her legs shake under the table. The damage is done, someone else knows everything.

Her mind becomes confused. She wants to be alone, far away from this commotion. She has only two meetings today, she can make the most of the soft spring sunlight for a few minutes' walk. She watches children playing on the swings in the Square du Temple. She was a child once too. Innocent, unaware, impatient as a teenager for what life had in store for her. Someone whistles at her. From the far side of the street a group of workmen are grinning as they watch her walk by. She stops for a moment opposite them, her head held high and her eyes steady. They quickly stop whistling. They can whistle at her, they can insult her, they can fuck her and they can rape her, but Marie will never change the way she is.

⋮

Laurent is in a deep sleep. Marie can hear his halting breathing and endless snoring, just like every morning. Lying there next to him, she can feel fever spreading through her body. She's falling sick at last, reacting physically to the stress. She gets the shakes so badly that Laurent eventually wakes up. "What's going on? Are you sick?" She tells him she's very cold. He puts his arms around her affectionately, runs a hand innocently over her pussy, his body spooned against hers. His fingers slowly ease into her wet vagina and fill Marie with a pleasure she hasn't experienced for a long time. The fever is making her delirious, she's no longer fully aware of anything, is getting close to a point of no return. She doesn't want to return; she'd like to stay in this infinite dark space, protected from madness by madness.

She's walking along the boulevard Voltaire alone, her every movement perfectly free. Rays of autumn sunshine project a lovely intense light on the facades of buildings. She takes the time to stop for a few minutes on the corner of an avenue to enjoy the pleasant warmth of it. She's just turning her face to the sky when she has the sudden sensation that the lower half of her body is going cold. She lowers her head slowly to look at the ground. There's blood flowing from her neck right down to her feet, her shoes are awash in hunks of liquid flesh stuck to the pavement. She doesn't move. Her breathing slows gradually, heavily. In the distance she can see the face of a man standing alone, watching her as she contorts on the ground in agony, and not offering her any help. It's Laurent. Roxane is with her mother and father, standing devastated on a balcony, screaming at Laurent, but he doesn't hear them. Marie is the only one who understands. They're telling him the truth. Their words horrify her and keep her pinned to the ground with no possibility of escape. She won't be able to get away and tell him that it's all lies. Laurent strains to listen but the screaming is inaudible to him. She still has some time. Marie struggles, soaking the sheets in sweat, rolls right into her husband's arms while also trying to shake them off. Laurent is still fondling her. He never stops touching her. She fights to stay in this unconscious state, to keep her eyes closed and stay in the dark waters of her imagination. Moans of pleasure mask her tears. Screams. The pleasure of her orgasm brings her out of the nightmare at the last minute.

Mathilde has stopped making eye contact with Marie. For several days now it's even felt as if she's avoiding her altogether. Marie has tried to talk to her a few times but she always came up with excuses to get away. Mathilde sent Marie an email a month ago to say that she'd prefer to work on projects alone rather than continuing with the partnerships the directors originally implemented. Their "transfer of skills" has failed. Marie has discussed this with Hervé but he didn't give her any advice, too preoccupied outwitting his wife's legal machinations in their divorce case. Their evening out the month before descended rapidly into a nightmare. His wife has met someone and wants to get remarried. She hasn't just had a fling that lasted a few days but has been leading a completely double life for more than eight years with another man from their neighborhood. She told Hervé that their marriage had only really worked for a few months. After that, she'd realized she'd already stopped loving him. Before making plans for a divorce she'd wanted to have a child with him so that she could get child support and benefit from some material comforts for a few years, while she made up her mind to start looking for work again. When they moved into the new house that Hervé had gone to the trouble of having built for them, Bernard was the first neighbor to welcome them to the area. "I could have imagined just about anyone, but not Bernard. He and I used to go fishing together on Sundays, we gathered up pigeon chicks that had fallen from their nests, and all those barbecues and birthdays, the parties. And the whole time he was fucking my wife. The worst of it is my own daughter knew about it and didn't say a word. In fact, she covered for them, the little bitch."

Marie doesn't want to disturb him with her problems. She's even planning to ask Laurent to represent Hervé in this shabby divorce case so that he can hold on to his assets. It would definitely be his only compensation.

After lunch, Marie receives an email from the director who is her immediate boss. She'd like to see her in her office at two o'clock sharp but gives no explanation. Marie decides to take all her current files with her, to be sure she isn't caught out. She knows her sales results for the last few weeks are bad. She's going to be reprimanded. She takes a deep breath and goes into her boss's office. Mathilde is sitting facing the director with her head lowered, she does not turn around. "Please come and sit down, Marie." The tone is abrupt, the atmosphere oppressive. Marie hates this windowless office, its only source of light a terrarium along one wall. Marie turns to look at Mathilde, trying to catch her eye for some explanation for their being here, but Mathilde keeps her head down.

The director turns to Marie first: "So, there seems to be a problem with the way your partnership is working. I'll make this quick because I have a meeting in a few minutes. You're going to stop working together because Mathilde has accused you of physical and psychological harassment. She came to see me a few days ago to complain about inappropriate physical contact made here at the bank, unsolicited messages, and violation of her private life. I can tell you that with just one week to go before we need to file our quarterly results, I don't really have time to deal with this sort of matter. You'd do better to inform Human Resources for them to take care of it, and get the trade union involved if need be. But for now, for the sake of stability at this branch and for the team as a whole, I must ask you to stop all contact. I'll assign you to different clients, so you won't have any files in common and won't have to communicate about anything, until we come up with a more workable solution. But perhaps you have other suggestions?"

Marie is stunned. She sits in silence, staring at a point on the floor. She must defend herself, but she can't get a single sound out of her mouth. Mathilde doesn't move, unshakable, sitting bolt upright on her chair. Marie flounders back up to the surface and tries to understand: "Harassment? What exactly are we talking about? I've never harassed anyone, never in my life!" Confronted with Mathilde's silence, Marie jumps to her feet and grabs her arm to shake it. Mathilde tries to protect herself. The director yells at them to stop immediately before she calls a security guard to separate them.

Mathilde shoves Marie back against the glass wall of the terrarium. A small potted palm tree collapses against the glass and Marie loses her balance. "You forcibly kissed me next to the printer! You followed me home to undress me and put me to bed, you exploited my weakness and the fact I'd split up with my boyfriend to get close to me. If you try anything again, anything, I'll file a complaint. Did you get that? Just one more thing and you'll end up in jail!"

The director asks Mathilde to leave the office and helps Marie to her feet. Marie grabs hold of the sleeve of her suit jacket. Clinging to the fabric she gazes at her pleadingly: "You know I didn't do anything. She's lying."

⋮

Two weeks off work. That's what
HR has recommended, until another
branch can take on Mathilde. The only reason Marie managed to hold on to her job
is that she has been with the bank a long
time. She hasn't dared tell Laurent what's
really behind all this. She's not sick and not
particularly depressed but told him she just
needed a few days' rest to get away from
her bosses' remonstrances about her weak
sales figures. And, as usual, Laurent believed his wife. Thomas now plays virtually no part at all in Marie's life. She has
renegotiated the contract with the day
nursery behind her husband's back, and
they now keep Thomas right through till
eight thirty. Sometimes Marie doesn't feel

like picking up her son after work. She wishes she could leave him to rot at the nursery. She'd abandon him there overnight if it were possible. Laurent asked his wife whether she would have Thomas at home for these two weeks, thinking it might cheer her up a little. She retorted tartly that she would rather not. She wants to make the most of this break from work on her own. He didn't press the point. Marie has had a dozen messages from Roxane, begging her to confess everything to Laurent straightaway. Marie never replies. She doesn't want to act in haste, with no concrete solution at hand.

Alone at the apartment, she tries to piece the whole story together, from the first time she met Mathilde to now. The director of Human Resources took the young woman's accusations very seriously, as good as forcing Marie to allow her access to her work emails and then to have a consultation with the psychiatrist employed by the company. The psychiatrist asked Marie how she felt about various examples of harassment, in both professional and private situations, and then asked her to remember any tiny details that could compromise her in this case. It all felt totally absurd to her. Surely Mathilde just wanted to take her job. The fact that she too was a victim of rape must be what triggered this whole fake harassment story.

The days go by with no real change. She gets up in the morning and goes to bed in the evening. Life is an eternity, nothing moves and nothing changes. It's easy to end up believing what everyone else believes. It occurs to Marie that she is part of a large organization, and that she personally contributes to the workings of a system that's now starting to betray her. When her maternity leave left her unfit to work on her own, she needed a partner, a double, a second younger, prettier Marie who could handle the client files and cope with new computer programs that she didn't understand. Marie was a mother, good for nothing: a womb, a vagina—but she had long since stopped being a woman. She sits on the sofa facing a big open window and can't imagine living any other way. This neighborhood she once so loved has become dull and lifeless. Like dead provincial streets where no one ever goes. It's like being on one of those endless roads, with no bends, no intersections, no possibility of escape, no alternatives. Where there's a feeling that everything's all mapped out already, where whatever happens—and usually nothing happens—you just have to stay within the lines and force yourself not to overstep them. Marie is now one of those people who just don't think. Her life is difficult, constrained, but that's simply the way it is. Now the only thing she's learning is hate.

:

I found this in the mailbox. What does it mean? Did the bank make you have a psychiatric assessment?" The mechanism is running amok, suddenly and for no reason deciding to dish out clues to her husband and family. She won't give in to panic. She's going to stay calm and, in a neutral voice, say that it was just a routine consultation as part of a public health campaign about harassment in the workplace. She chooses her words as if someone else were dictating them to her. Laurent doesn't ask any more questions but says she has every right to refuse to comply with this sort of thing on the grounds of patient confidentiality. Marie feels like laughing out loud, but clenches her jaw and balls her fists to avoid showing the beginnings of a smile. She knows better than anyone about patient confidentiality. She ends the conversation by kissing her husband and making him promise never to open her mail again without her consent. If it's franked by the bank it's always for her, better to be absolutely clear on that.

On Mondays Marie always feels as if she's come home from vacation and is going back to work. Before getting to the office she drops Thomas at the day nursery. While she was off sick, Laurent's mother insisted on having the child for a full week. Marie made sure the nursery staff believed she herself had been alone with her son for the whole period. She doesn't know why she lies. Lying feels good to her, unburdens her of her reality. She never finds the courage to be directly honest, preferring to lie a little before revealing the truth through a number of minor details. Making a lie plausible is a complicated business. There must be no slipups.

The new nursery director introduces herself to Marie: "I'm Brigitte Renate. I wanted to have a word this morning. Do you have time for a coffee? Just five minutes." She's a heavy lady and she doesn't let go of Marie's hand or stop staring into her eyes. Marie knows she has no choice and agrees to go with her. Unlike the other mothers, she's never been beyond the lobby. She always waits on the sofa until a member of the staff brings Thomas to her at the agreed time. She's been invited to have a look around the nursery several times and to go into the playroom to see her son but she couldn't do it. The smell brought back too many bad memories: the disinfectant wipes they used at the maternity unit, the smell of warm milk, the rustle of plastic antibacterial overshoes. In the corridor, about a hundred children's drawings are displayed alongside public health posters about vaccinations and the dangers of flu for newborns. The doors are decorated with big stickers of daisies and teddy bears. Marie knows that everyone at the center likes talking about her. She hears whispering and muttering, sees the faces and false smiles.

The nursery director makes her a coffee in her office. Marie sits in her chair as if about to have her final interview for the Mommy of the Year awards. The coffee scalds her lips satisfyingly. Brigitte Renate is bulky and imposing, a strikingly large woman. But after the first few minutes of their conversation everything falls apart. Her physical presence is erased by her moral weakness. Her big, overly obvious, hypocritical smile, her hands crossed ridiculously on her desk, her screwed-up eyes, and her fat cheeks encroaching over her lower lids. The woman has no subtlety whatsoever. She isn't intelligent, and even less shrewd. She won't do Marie any harm. "I'm so sorry but I'm only here in the mornings so it's not easy arranging meetings. I'd just like to get to know you a little, know a bit about Thomas's home environment. Find out if you have any particular requirements or needs, whether you're satisfied. Some of the mothers say that maybe you don't feel entirely comfortable here...What I mean is, you mustn't be afraid to come into the nursery, you know...We're here for you..."

Marie interrupts her to say she's always in a hurry when she gets here in the evenings and doesn't have time to lie down on Thomas's playmat or make a scene about him putting round balls into square holes. Her husband is a leading lawyer who works day and night on his cases. She takes care of Thomas alone, bathing him, feeding him, soothing him, putting him to bed. The director listens to her, makes a show of understanding her. She doesn't express this very clearly, though, and perhaps that's the worst of it, the feeling that this woman is demonstrating an earnest sort of condolence, which is in fact simply a profound contempt for the sort of mother Marie represents. In response to Marie's abrupt and almost aggressive tone of voice, the director cuts short their conversation and shows her back to the door. She thanks Marie for sparing her some time and is available if and when she's needed. Marie smiles by way of acquiescence. She opens the door and then thinks again. "Oh, and is Thomas okay?" The director assures her that he's absolutely fine and has already settled in the playroom. Marie is making more and more mistakes.

Marie knows that she now needs to get things under control. First her mother, then her sister, Mathilde, and the day nursery…and soon Laurent. The world of lies is closing in around her. She's terrified and desperate, a slow-moving tension seeping into every corner of her mind. She finally recognizes that this is the thrill of an abnormal life.

:

Marie acknowledges that it's never a good thing for a woman to stop making love with her husband. It's difficult and laborious but she's decided to make the necessary effort so that he believes everything's still possible. She caresses him slowly but he can't get an erection. His limp penis curled on his thigh repulses her. Laurent always chooses the reaction most common to men, the one that works every time, arousing compassion and pity in their partners, who always feel responsible for the situation: victimization. He peels her away from his chest and sits up on the edge of the bed with his clenched hands at his temples and his head bent, heaving great sighs of despair—she isn't spared any part of the performance. "I think I'm working too much. This case is driving me nuts. When it's all over we'll go away for a vacation. The three of us. Get away from all this." Marie knows he's been under a lot of pressure for several weeks. During the preliminary inquiries into the Ponce case he's received almost twenty death threats at work, and ten of them were addressed specifically to him; he's been sent big bags filled with cow brains with promises that next time it will be his brains inside, pigs' trotters sent in parcels, and fake tongues in small boxes.

But Marie's instincts tell her this isn't just about difficulties at work. For days now she's felt the presence of "the other woman." The mistress, the whore, the unmentionable, the bitch, the woman who destroys, lays waste, and undermines a married couple's often shaky foundations. It's always smell that betrays an unfaithful man. Laurent falls asleep quickly and Marie sniffs his body, licks the crook of his neck and studies his hair and his hands on the pillow. Nothing exists anymore except in her own imagination. She suddenly feels Laurent is defying her. He's cheating on her with Julia, and lying to her too. They must both navigate these treacherous waters to the best of their abilities. Marie turns to the other side of the bed. The walls of her vagina contract painfully and her hips sway slightly from left to right.

Her husband has always liked her masturbating when they have sex; he likes seeing her play with herself for him alone. Doing this during sex has never given Marie any pleasure. Her husband's hand was always over hers, encouraging her to rub herself. Her sexual activity as a teenager, even when she was a virgin, felt more independent than what she does now within her marriage. Like all young girls, when she took a bath Marie had gotten into the habit of turning on the shower and putting the showerhead up to her vagina. The water pressure was too weak but she would put her hand on it to create more pressure and make the water jets stronger. She would always achieve orgasm, with no help at all. Once a woman emerges from this solitary space—when she has little knowledge of sex between two or more people—her sex life rapidly grows more complex. With so much promise intensified by the erotic power of the sexual act between a man and a woman, the guilt of not achieving gratification is a depressing outcome. It was a genuine disappointment for Marie when she realized, on the first and many subsequent occasions, that a penis penetrating her didn't give her as much pleasure as her showerhead in Bois-le-Roi. Male sexuality—with its lack of promise, originality, and scope—just kept disappointing her, from her marriage right up to her rape. Perhaps she even had some sort of fellow feeling for her rapist, who recognized the violence of sex and allowed himself to apply it deliberately to innocent women, thereby refusing to be trapped in the sexual routines imposed on him by his marriage. His penis was hard. Harder than her husband's has ever been for her. She remembers him ramming powerfully deep inside her, bucking savagely against her back. Marie sometimes regrets that there could be no communion with that man, that she couldn't experience a pleasure that would have been appropriate for their two suffering bodies, the one frustrated, the other subjugated. She could have become something other than his victim, and he something other than her tormentor. She mulls over all sorts of ambiguous ideas tonight, immoral considerations, sick introspection, titillating thoughts, dismissing and then reappraising them from every possible angle. Cars speed past on the boulevard outside, their tires thundering relentlessly over the road surface. And it's his proud body that she feels quivering with every urge, his face she sees lying beside her.

Little Thomas is sick, he's quite a fragile child. He can't cope with his mother's abandonment. Marie has to stay at home with him. She sacrifices her one day off a month for him. He's been screaming in his bed for several minutes and Marie has shut herself in her room so she doesn't have to listen to his wailing. She'll take his temperature when she gives him his bottle, killing two birds with one stone. That'll be less effort, less time devoted to him.

She's lying on her bed looking for her cell phone. She's sure she left it on the nightstand last night. There's absolutely no need for panic. Now that her sister knows about things, she's deleted the letter to Laurent from her computer, changed the access code on her cell, and wiped all the compromising messages she's exchanged with Roxane. The screaming is more intense in the corridor. A strong smell of urine and excrement fills the living room. Marie walks past her son without a glance, obsessed with finding her phone. She spots it on the small shelf near the front door. She's never left it there. She very clearly remembers checking her emails before going to sleep. Laurent has taken to searching, watching her, trying things out, putting his doubts into action.

The child won't stop howling. Marie consents to change his diaper and give him something to eat. There's nothing she finds more disgusting than watching her son have his bottle. The milky smells—so sour and sweet and warm—make her feel permanently nauseous. She hasn't drunk a single drop of milk herself since Thomas was born. He guzzles it down like a pig. He hasn't eaten since yesterday evening.

There are times when her negligence becomes apparent again. Marie may take care of Thomas for several consecutive days as normal mothers do and a routine is established. But the following week she lets him starve, flail in his own excrement, suddenly feeling an urge to make him eat it, to hurl him out of the window, thrilled and satisfied by the thought that she can finally get him out of her life. She wavers between the energy it takes to sustain her lie and the unbearable exhaustion driving her toward ending it all as soon as possible.

After her rape, Marie always thought of herself as the only victim in this masquerade, of this fabrication that the whole world keeps afloat about the incredible enriching experience of motherhood. Despite how weak her body was when she gave birth, Marie did not fight for her son but against him. She didn't completely abandon her body in the hospital. It would have been unimaginable for her to die bringing him into the world. As she struggled on that bed destined to see him born into suffering, she made a commitment to make him pay the price his entire life. If only one person could be saved, she would naturally have chosen herself.

The bell on the intercom rings. Marie has fallen asleep on the sofa. The child is clinging to her leg, chewing on the fabric of her pants. Laurent forgot his keys. He's home early. She won't raise the subject of her cell phone this evening. She'd rather wait till she knows exactly how far his suspicions have developed over the last few days.

⠸

Roxane does not intend to leave
her in peace, picking away at her like a vul-
ture with its prey. Waiting for her to snap. A
dull clunk reverberates in the apartment but
is smothered by her sister's yelling.

"What exactly do you want? The truth
about Thomas? You think he can take it?
I hate you, I can't understand why you're
not on my side. My own sister and you're
betraying me."

The conversation becomes increasingly
spiteful. The slats of the parquet floor creak
underfoot. Marie is screaming with fury,
she hurls the handset of the phone at the
wall, then calls her sister back to apologize.
A door closes behind her. Marie sobs, begs
her sister not say anything to her mother

or Laurent, asks her to understand her situation. Their voices subside, the intensity defuses. A second door closes discreetly. Marie stops talking, takes the phone from her ear. She steps slowly toward the corridor to check that no one has come into the apartment. Laurent has a business lunch today. The guy in the apartment below must be doing more renovations.

Julia is an attentive coworker. "Where's submissions file number eight? Don't tell me you left it at home again." Laurent has to drive back to the apartment before his lunch. His wife has stopped reminding him to take his files. He knows exactly where this file is: on the windowsill in the living room. He has just a few minutes to grab it before heading back to the restaurant near the Bois de Boulogne, where Julia and their client are waiting for him. The Ponce case is on the homestretch. This highly publicized divorce will guarantee him not only a promotion within his law firm, but perhaps also recognition among all the top Paris institutions in political, media, and legal circles.

He comes into the apartment and hears his wife on the phone. As soon as he starts walking down the corridor a terrible sense of fear grips him, as if he can feel the first tremors of a huge earthquake under his feet. Marie's harrowing ranting echoes around the apartment. He comes slowly toward the bedroom. The phone is thrown at the wall. There's a few seconds' silence before his wife starts whimpering as she tries to resume her conversation with her sister. He can see her through the half-open doorway, kneeling on the white carpet by the bed. Her every word pierces through his chest. The bitter acidic taste of his morning coffee rises up his throat, filling the back of his mouth and infiltrating his nose. He closes the door carefully and goes back down the corridor. He races downstairs, shouldering past the caretaker who's sweeping the stairs. He doesn't apologize. He doesn't need to apologize for anything. There aren't many possible lies when it comes to a man and his son. Thomas looks like him.

The GPS in the car is already set and tells him the way. "Starting route to La Grande Cascade." He stops listening to the automatic voice, gets lost in northern Paris. Makes a U-turn. First he wants to go see his son at the nursery but apparently they have an outing planned for the children today. Marie always gives him this sort of information at the last minute, as he sets off to work. His shirt is patched with acrid sweat, every fiber of his clothes clings to his skin, embedding itself in his flesh. His eyes roam over the paths through the Bois de Boulogne. The road becomes hazy, anger burns through his body like a slow painful electric shock. How could his wife cheat on him? He can't believe Thomas isn't his son. It's just impossible. Only last week he and his mother were looking at photos and comparing his features to Thomas's. His head feels heavy and his hands are losing their grip on the steering wheel. The car grinds to a halt by the roadside. He steps out, shaking feverishly with terror. He, the lawyer who specializes in tragic personal defense speeches, can't stand being ill-prepared to confront an ordeal. His body gives way. Slumped against the car door, he stares absently at the far horizon of the woods stretching out before him. A few walkers eye him suspiciously from a distance. His phone vibrates in his pocket. It's Julia. He needs to get to the restaurant right now and bring the file he forgot at home. Everyone's there except for him. After the tenth call, still collapsed by the roadside, he makes up his mind to reply. He's real close. It's just that there's an accident on the way into the woods. He's lying, like his wife. A lie to defend himself, to avoid annoying people, to make them more amenable, more flexible, to achieve some sweet peaceful serenity until, someday, he has the courage to reveal everything. His suit is spattered with large patches of puke. Luckily, he has another one in the trunk of the car.

．
．
．

Hey look, Thomas, Daddy came today!" Unlike his wife, Laurent didn't think twice before putting on the blue plastic overshoes to go into the nursery's playroom. The director is delighted to meet little Thomas's father. They chat, discussing the child's progress, his interactions with the other children, his ability to orient himself and his sense of space. When Marie gets home after picking him up, she lets him roam around the apartment alone. He rolls about, lies spread-eagle on all the carpets, trundles around between cushions on the floor, navigates alone and unprotected between the pieces of furniture in the living room while his mother reads in her bedroom or does something in the kitchen.

Laurent can't help scrutinizing his son. His big smiling green eyes, his little pink mouth grinning up at him, his tiny nose that twists from left to right. He can't be certain anymore, the doubt is devastating. What if this child isn't his? He needs to be sure. Laurent is a man of the law. He likes having tangible proof in front of him, real material evidence. He's never pictured his life anywhere but grounded in reality. He has no problem with spending his nights cramming hundreds of pages of witness reports, inventories, minutes of meetings, lists, assessments of proof, and images of adulterous encounters. Even as a teenager he was already aware of powerful boundaries. While his classmates started going to discos, drinking, and experimenting with all sorts of drugs, he was shackled by his fear of the possible consequences. These heavy restrictions—which instigate justice and are in fact open to very little negotiation—have always been a source of comfort to him with their guarantee that nothing can ever be completely repealed or deconstructed. Only a civil war would be reason enough for Laurent to lose this equanimity. He has used lies in several of his cases but that was more a question of professional strategy.

He moves away with his child in his arms. Thomas looks at him and then turns to look outside. Laurent assembles, reconstructs, and juxtaposes recent and older events. He comes very close, then backs away. Some things are inconsistent with the rest. The expressions that sometimes come into his wife's face cast an unbearable ambiguity over moments from their everyday life. Past and present become intertwined. But he can't seem to establish a possible link. He is so caught up in his own convictions that he can't detect the initial tragedy.

Marie has made the most of her free evening by going to the hairdresser. "Don't you like it? You haven't said a thing." Laurent assures her that it's a great success, sensibly limiting his compliments. He doesn't have the heart to go into action but would rather study his wife's behavior before making a decision.

Marie is going to cook lasagna this evening. All the fresh vegetables are sitting on the counter in the kitchen. In their old apartment, before they were married, Laurent and Marie used to love cooking together. They would huddle up close and concoct a single dish between the two of them, then enjoy it with a lot of love and a good bottle of red wine. It's things like this that still nudge Laurent toward believing in his wife. The lost memories, the buried passion, and the forgotten promises. But there is palpable doubt in the unbreathable air in this household. Something has been broken, as when the first fights break out. Love is fresh and happy. The man and the woman adore each other, make love several times a day, promise each other not only eternity but the impossible. Then comes the first raised voice, a tiny harbinger of separation in a flash of anger or a judgment. And the other person's impetuous character is gradually revealed in all its vices and idiosyncrasies, the surface image is shattered. The lovers no longer have the same energy in their passionate embraces, they stop making love, distance themselves as much as possible from each other. It's happening to them too. Laurent suspects his wife, Marie loathes her husband for not understanding anything even though she herself is doing her utmost to hide the biggest crisis of their lives.

Thomas is sitting at the table with them this evening. Laurent has insisted that he be up on the same level as them for the meal. They're all together. The intercom rings. "Let it ring, it must be a delivery man or a neighbor who's forgotten their key." Laurent doesn't contradict Marie. A few minutes later their own doorbell rings. Laurent gets up to open the door. Marie recognizes her sister's voice through the kitchen's thin walls. Roxane is breathless, standing panting in the hallway, supported by Laurent who kindly invites her to join them for dinner. With Roxane's every footstep over the parquet in the corridor, Marie's fingers tense on her paper napkin. She didn't invite her sister over

this evening. Roxane appears in the doorway. Marie
manages a brief forced smile for Laurent's sake. Usually, he would finish his food quickly to leave the two
women to talk, but the conversation he overheard yesterday means he needs to stay on the alert. This impromptu visit might be his chance to discover the truth
at last.

Marie embarks on a conversation about the birthday present she bought for her father. Roxane is visibly
uncomfortable, she'd like to admit the full extent of
what she knows straightaway. She could turn to Laurent and tell him everything her sister has done. She
wouldn't have the courage. She's paralyzed by the look
in Marie's eyes. Filtered through her story about buying
this present is all the terror and violence of a woman
who now knows she's being hunted down. Laurent
watches her but doesn't see anything. He loves his
wife. And in this state of turbulence he can't possibly
spot the mistake. He's a tired husband, an exhausted
husband, overwhelmed by the weight of suspicion.

Laurent leaves the table and Marie struggles to disguise her relief. She's not always sufficiently aware of
the weaknesses in her loved ones. Roxane will never
manage to tell Laurent the truth. She's too frightened.
Whereas Laurent is still governed by his love for her.
He won't be able to do a thing. And the child will be no
help to him. His body spoke only once and since then

Marie has been vigilant about her son's cleanliness, even if that meant changing him with her eyes closed or leaving him in the bath without really watching over him. In fact, now that she's facing her sister alone, she's no longer afraid of losing this battle. In some instances, the victims determine the future course of action. And that is what she allows to happen.

"I just came to say you're right. This is your problem. It's up to your conscience but don't expect me to keep helping you with your lies. That's over." Her sister's pity extends only to Thomas and Laurent. Marie feels she made the right decision by choosing silence after she was raped. Her sister hasn't even asked her who her rapist was. Not for a moment has the subject of the sexual assault been referred to directly by Roxane. Her mother hasn't asked any questions either. When she found her own daughter swimming in filth, she didn't even have it in her to ask for explanations. The facts were enough. The consequences visible and irreparable. Ever cautious, they're all acting in silence. The rape is vanishing under the weight of more recent events. Its gnawing, degraded violence is called into question in various ways and simply eclipses itself from the surface of this torment and sorrow. And they each start out on their lives again.

:

Paul doesn't understand: "A test? Are you sure that's what you want? You can't turn the clock back afterward." Laurent is sure. He won't back down. He explains his suspicions about his wife, all her strange behavior since Thomas was born, her endless lies that he's discovered in the last few days. Paul is surprised and thinks privately that, at the end of the day, no one ever really knows what goes on within a couple. The tensions, emotions, infidelities, their relationships with their child—all things that are camouflaged, prettified, wrapped up in a sweet sugary coating to hide the bitterness deep in the heart of the whole setup.

Laurent couldn't get to sleep last night. As he lay next to his wife, the bed felt so deep and heavy. He feels he's sinking into something whose contours he still can't make out clearly, trying to stay afloat, struggling to understand, going over and over events in his mind. The two of them taking Thomas for a stroll along the Canal de l'Ourcq. He remembers watching tourists as they walked by or cheerfully clinked glasses on moored barges, the flat greenish water, the big restaurant terraces outside the Rotonde Stalingrad building full of people and flooded with sunlight. It's like a freeze-frame with this peaceful setting stretching to the horizon. A floating feeling wraps him in clammy warmth. He can see his wife in the distance. Standing upright and holding Thomas's buggy confidently. They're close to the water. She's rocking the buggy slowly backward and forward. Its wheels slide on the paving slabs at the water's edge. This clearly etched image of his wife and son could be his last before the drama. He'll never see them again. The buggy is only a couple of inches from falling into the canal's black depths. Laurent can feel his heart beating; he comes slowly over to Marie. She senses him behind her, turns around. Her eyes are filled with grief. She wanted to do it, was prepared to go through with it. They continued with their walk along the dock. Laurent remembers that afternoon, remembers all these little details that now look like great daubs of blue paint on his wife's guilty face.

Paul explains the procedure for a paternity test. It's not difficult to carry out. There are dozens of Web sites that offer mail-order kits but Laurent came to Paul to be sure he would have no unpleasant surprises. Marie won't know anything about this, and he will have his friend's support if it turns out that Thomas isn't his biological son.

The two men say their goodbyes sadly. Paul feels bad for Laurent. He knows the dramas that extramarital affairs can cause. A few years after his own wedding he met a nurse on night duty at the hospital. They often met up at work, had passionate trysts on the hospital premises, and then Paul would go home with the satisfaction of having a personal life as varied and intense as his work. But the nurse ended up wanting more. More dates, more outings, more dinners and weekends together. She pestered Paul with insulting messages, threats, ultimatums, and declarations of her love. Sophia eventually found out about the whole thing. Paul begged her to forgive him and swore he would never do it again. Sophia forgave him. She even arranged to meet the desperate young woman to ask her to stop pursuing her husband.

Confronted with a man's infidelity, a woman often feels thoroughly ashamed. Laurent has also been tempted by Julia. One evening after work she suggested they have one last drink at her place to celebrate their progress on the Ponce case. Laurent wavered. His mind was already tying itself in knots, weighing up the pros and cons, gauging the good and the bad in what he was about to do. He declined. He very much wanted to but the consequences were too onerous. He didn't want any problems with Marie, was keen to stay comfortably nestled in his home, surrounded by his family, and wouldn't take even the smallest risk of losing everything.

Laurent has gotten into the habit of picking up Thomas in the evenings, and Marie is delighted to have more time to herself at the end of the day. Today she's decided to go to the movies with Sophia, making the most of this rare period of calm. Which is Laurent's opportunity to act. Paul gave him a small bag with everything he needs to carry out the paternity test: latex gloves, four long cotton swabs, two plastic tubes, and the instructions. Thomas is quiet and Laurent watches him in the rearview mirror. He's not sure. Even if Thomas isn't his son, he loves him as if he were his own. A driver sounds his horn. Laurent hurries back to the apartment and settles his son in the bathroom. He tears open the packaging. Thomas twists his head in every direction. It's difficult to get the swab into his mouth because he refuses to open his lips. Laurent sees himself in the mirror: his gloved hands carefully holding the two long swabs, then slipping them into the phials before sealing the pouch. He hopes Thomas will never remember this, that the poor child will forget all the doubts weighing down on his head. Before Marie comes home he has time to drop the test off at Paul's office. He doesn't want to run any unnecessary risks by keeping it at home. Paul has told him it should take about three days. The hospital will let him know when the results are ready.

Laurent feels relieved. He managed to go through with it. Only his son could make him doubt his decision. But the child seems to give his assent with just one look.

⋮

It's Marie's father's birthday and the whole family has gathered at Bois-le-Roi to celebrate, as they do every year. Irene has decorated the table sumptuously and prepared a delicious meal, ending with a big cake that she ordered in advance from the patisserie.

Roxane hasn't spoken a word to Marie since her impromptu visit to her apartment. Their mother thinks this is just a routine tiff between the two women, about children or work. Roxane looks away every time Marie comes near.

Laurent is bouncing Thomas on his lap on the sofa. He wants to be happy today before tragedy strikes. He can't imagine what lies in store if the test is negative. A future without Marie, without his son, without this warm and loving family in Bois-le-Roi. A future made up of nothing. Wandering alone around the law firm, drowning in work and heartbreak, he would be lost. He would have nothing. Laurent has never tried to judge his marriage objectively. Their day-to-day life—with its innocent little arguments about a crooked tooth-paste cap or an empty toilet paper holder—doesn't bother him. Comforting habits have a pleasant anes-thetic effect, and that's where the danger lies. But a man without such habits is lost. Perhaps Laurent won't tell his wife the truth.

Marie brings in two dishes of deviled eggs that her mother has arranged attractively in staggered rows. The rest of the meal is gargantuan. A woman who spends so long cooking on her own isn't usually a very happy one; in most instances this is just a way of forgetting everything else. Marie has stopped fighting. Sitting in the living room opposite Roxane and her husband, she feels she's claimed victory. Everything's falling per-fectly back into place. Irene asks the whole family to come sit at the table, and Roxane makes a point of sit-ting as far from Marie as possible.

Laurent feels he's in a privileged position. "Come on then, Laurent, tell us about this case. How's it going?" In Laurent's opinion, the significant media coverage of the Ponce case in the last few days has been over the top. It's only a divorce suit. "Yes, but there's also the rape of that girl." Silence settles over the room. Roxane couldn't help speaking out. It was overpowering. Marie stares at her from the other end of the table with a reproachful smile. She utterly loathes her. Can't understand why this once loving and empathetic sister is now determined to do her so much harm. She needs some air, makes her excuses, and leaves the table.

As a teenager she spent whole afternoons reading and daydreaming in the conservatory. She never complained, but she often felt the heavy burden of someone who's never experienced anything exceptional. No suffering, no problems with family, finances, or relationships. No sickness and no deaths. She grew up in this healthy united family that gave her the values she would pass on to her own children. There were never any obstacles in her life until the rape. She knows that a woman who's lived with poverty and depravity, hunger and death, hatred and violence might not have reacted in the same way. She would have had the courage to report this crime, to run away and have an abortion. She wouldn't have hidden everything behind appearances. This realization makes Marie feel sick to her stomach.

When Laurent doesn't come home until late in the evening, she sometimes goes onto Internet forums. Sites with daily posts from women who've been beaten, raped, and sexually assaulted. Marie has never

participated in these conversations. She's never succeeded in doing it, not even under cover of anonymity.
Some of the women kept their rapist's child, and they
talk about this. In some cases, the child can even see its
father freely with no judgment spoiling these visits. Situations are normalized to make them more bearable.
Marie could talk about what happened to her. But the
consequences would be disastrous for her marriage, her
family, and her work. She'd lose everything. Her CEO
is a rapist but also a discreet and sensitive husband, a
father who cares about his two daughters' upbringing,
and head of a banking group with excellent business
results. When she climbed out of his car he threatened
to destroy her marriage and her career if she talked.
But the child will talk one day. Marie will confess her
whole story to Thomas. The culprit definitely won't be
punished. The case will be closed.

Marie surfaces from her thoughts. There's a phone
vibrating on the table in the veranda where they had
their aperitifs. She recognizes her husband's cell. He
left it on the table. She goes over to pick it up and take
it to him. A long message lights up on the home screen.
It's an email. Without the phone's access code, Marie
can see only the beginning. "Dear sir, the results of the
paternity test you carried out on June 16, 2014, at the
laboratories of the Pitié-Salpêtrière University Hospital,
will be available on Thursday, June 19, 2014, from..."

She holds her breath. Reality distorts around her. The phone quivers in her shaking hand. In the end she puts it down. She's stunned. How could he have done the test behind her back?

She wonders about her sister and her mother. There's a slight risk they've spoken to him. And there's her CEO. Could Laurent have seen him? Does he know everything? She throws herself at Laurent's phone but can't unlock it. She tries several combinations of numbers. Without success. She can hear her husband laughing in the dining room and discreetly moves closer to spy on the familiar faces of those she suspects are guilty. Thomas is sitting in his high chair. As usual, his grandmother has given him a sugared toy to help with his teething. Laurent is playing with him, taking the toy from him and then handing it back and smothering his face with kisses. Roxane is walled up in silence. Her mother is talking to her but she's not listening. Her husband Julien is having to take an interest in his mother-in-law's conversation and to answer on his wife's behalf. Only Marie's father looks relaxed. He's celebrating his seventieth birthday, surrounded by his family. He has no worries to fret over anymore. His life is quiet, peaceful, and private. A great wave of anxiety washes over Marie. Laurent will soon know the truth. He won't react the same way as Roxane. Silence won't be an acceptable solution for him. He'll make decisions.

Throw her out with just a few clothes, tell her family, her friends, her coworkers, even have her forcibly interned in a psychiatric unit by a friend of Paul's. Paul. She'd forgotten about him. Is he responsible for this? Did he have his doubts when Laurent told him about Marie's behavior and reactions? She'll call Sophia. Tomorrow. No, after lunch. The sooner the better.

Her mind fogs over. She loses her balance. A vase on the windowsill shatters at her feet. "Marie? Is everything okay?" her mother calls from the dining room. She uses her hands to scrape up the shards scattered over the floor. Tears stream down her cheeks. Her mother hurries over to her. "Marie, stop it! Stop it! I'll get the broom. Don't touch it, it's sharp." Marie's body tips backward slightly. Laurent watches from where he's sitting. He has Thomas in his arms. Marie studies him for a moment. A stab of pain distracts her but she can't take her eyes off her husband. She wants to beg him to stop. The floor is dotted with drops of blood. Her palm is cut right across, with partially visible fragments of glass buried in her flesh.

Her husband hastily puts Thomas into his buggy and runs over to her. "What are you doing? Come, we need to disinfect it." A long trail of blood trickles onto the white tiled floor in the living room. As she walks through the dining room, Marie sees Roxane at the table. She's finishing her helping of cake. Marie thinks she makes out a slight smile. Laurent hurries her along. He opens drawers in the bathroom, looking for dressings. Irene appears. "Is everything okay? Do you think I should call a doctor? It does look deep." Laurent says he can handle it. Irene goes to clear up the mess on the veranda. Laurent tries to extract the larger pieces of glass with tweezers. Marie screams in pain. Perhaps he thinks she deserves it. She'd be happier swallowing the glass so there could be no more words. Properly grinding up all these shards and ramming great handfuls of them into her body. She'd be overrun with glass.

Laurent doesn't react to her cries. Marie stares at him the whole time as he plucks out the tiny glinting fragments. Her hand looks like a map of muscle tissue. A hundred different possibilities come into her sick mind. Husband and wife take refuge in silence.

Before finally looking away she asks, "Did you like the meal?"

⋮

Marie finds the nights go on forever. There's only one day left before Laurent finds out the truth. Every thought becomes a trial as she strives for an effective solution. She spent last night on Internet forums looking for a way to end it all. With no success. She's overtired. Her body registers nothing but exhaustion and sadness. What she finds most difficult is seeing the child every day. She wants him to disappear from her life. Laurent is becoming increasingly suspicious of her. She caught him one evening scrolling through her cell phone and rifling through her coat pockets. They avoid each other in the apartment, trying their best to hide their discomfort.

At the bank Marie can't deal with her workload, her coworkers have turned their backs on her since the accusation of harassment, she's losing her people skills. She can't cope anymore. Once she leaves work there are still all those women with buggies, all those kids playing and those couples holding hands in the street. Little details that disgust her, make her feel nauseous. She's tormented by anxiety. Only one day left. Just one day. That's so little. The vast ocean of the lie is closing in around her. Once everyone knows about her rape she'll never have a normal life again. Judged, disparaged for her silence, humiliated by those around her. It all needs to go away, and fast. The proof, the facts, the consequences, the emotions, the bodies. The bodies. She needs to bring this whole thing to an end herself. No one will do it for her. The restaurant terrace is full of people. Marie squeezes her thighs, her stomach, her breasts. She thinks about a body's content, how it re-acts to things. She feels ready to resolve everything. All life has to offer her is total submission, a protracted decline from which she'll never recover. The solutions ran out long ago already. When she climbed out of that car she felt a part of her mind leave her. She couldn't re-constitute the facts, pick up the coherent thread of her life, and when she told people she was pregnant that battle came to an end. Thomas, the child who brought about her downfall. His every cry deserves death, but all it produces in her is a profound exasperation at her own impotence. In a few hours' time she'll finally be able to reach an effective decision.

A woman sitting near her complains of a stomach-ache. "I think I'm getting my period. It's always like this." The woman's friend takes a small red-and-white sachet from her bag and tells her to take the medication to ease the pain. She rips the sachet open and pours the contents into her glass. The powder dissolves in the water, forming little white bubbles on the surface. The woman feels better already. Thomas will feel even better. The woman smiles as she drinks the strange-colored mixture and then thuds the glass down on the table. Laurent always puts his glass down like that, as if rapping the table with his fist. Their destinies are becoming clear. Marie thinks about the fates of her loved ones, and doesn't fight off the terrible thoughts coming into her mind. She just accepts that this is the logical conclusion to the story.

．
．
．

She'll never go back to the bank. For this afternoon, Marie claims she doesn't feel so well, she has a slight fever. Her director gives her permission to go home. As she leaves the premises on the place de la République for the last time she feels a huge wave of relief. The long years spent in this organization never afforded her any real recognition. She just contributed to the smooth running of it all. She's already stopped thinking about it. The future no longer exists. Plans, stress about the days ahead, arranging vacations, afternoons at Bois-le-Roi, potential arguments—none of it matters anymore. The Métro doors close with a long *bing* sound. The carriages reek of filth and piss. She won't smell this anymore.

A man stares at Marie from the opposite platform. He doesn't know where she's heading or what she's going to do in a few hours' time. He doesn't recognize her suffering or her satisfaction. It's a premeditated act.

This morning Marie hunted down some prescriptions Paul had given her to help her with stress and exhaustion after Thomas was born. Two boxes of Zopiclone to help her sleep, two boxes of Lexomil to calm her nerves, along with some milder drugs that never had any effect. Marie didn't like taking these drugs. They often put her in an unpleasant state, a combination of well-being and profound anxiety. She experienced both emotions at the same time: a feeling that she was perfectly attuned to her situation while being aware of the completely artificial effects that tranquilizers have on depressive patients. Three or four of the prescriptions hadn't been stamped by pharmacies but were old and no longer valid. It took Marie only a few hours to falsify the dates with the help of a digital retouching program. Laurent was always pretty much against her taking these drugs and she didn't have the strength to insist, so she'd just stowed the prescriptions among her things until the day came when they'd be useful.

The Fifteenth Arrondissement is a neutral neighborhood. There's no one out walking through the Boucicaut area. When she comes out of the Métro, Marie heads down the wide avenue Félix-Faure. The change of environment throws her, but the first pharmacy she comes to gives her confidence: it's big and full of people. She has no trouble obtaining the drugs. In the rush and stress of the store no one notices the falsified date on the prescription. After a few words of advice about how frequently to take the medication and the fatal consequences of combining it with alcohol, the two little boxes of tranquilizers are carefully packed into a bag for her. She crosses to the other side of the street where there's a second pharmacy. Three boxes of sleeping pills are handed over. It's quite the medical treasure hunt. Not one of the pharmacists notices the date stamps. She can reuse her prescriptions twice. Back on the Métro, sitting on a fold-down seat, she has the equivalent of ten boxes of drugs in all varieties.

She stops at Saint-Lazare station to go to the large home improvements and gardening store that she located on the Internet. It's two in the afternoon. The huge space is dotted with customers wandering up and down the wide aisles. Sales staff hurry busily here and there. Marie doesn't want to waste any time. "Hello. I need some antifreeze for car radiators." Third aisle on the left. The product is in her basket. A fair-haired young man is giving a customer advice about the merits of a set of plastic washers for bathrooms. Marie waits for him to finish before approaching: "Hi, I'm looking for rat poison." She can feel the excitement and anxiety at the sound of her own words. He stares at her for a moment. Marie is unsettled by this brief silence. Can he tell what she's planning? "What sort of rodent is it for? And do you live in a house or an apartment?" The questions surprise her. She hasn't met any obstacles so far. She explains that it's not for her but her parents. They have a large house in the country and they've found about a dozen rats among their things in the attic. The salesman smiles at her, nods politely and takes her to the right department to hand her the product. He gives her some information about the danger of ingesting rat poison. She thanks him warmly for all his recommendations and goes off to the checkout counter to pay.

It's now three in the afternoon. Marie is just relieved. She spills her day's shopping onto the table. She's going to cook for the whole rest of the afternoon: osso buco for the main course followed by chocolate mousse, and stewed apple for Thomas. She'll have time to get it all ready before Laurent comes home. She's stopped feeling anxious now. Last night she trawled through dozens of Internet sites to research the effects of each combination. She read hundreds of warnings about toxic products. The antifreeze and the rat poison will be the most effective in view of Thomas's body weight. With Laurent it will be a more complex undertaking. He's bigger and heavier. The sleeping pills will have an immediate effect but the poison is bound to take longer. Marie is banking on the absence of medical treatment for several hours after the poison is ingested, to help her achieve her aim.

She inherited a marble pestle and mortar from her grandmother. She's never used it for fear of damaging it. Each sheet contains fourteen pills. She still has several unopened boxes left. Sleeping pills, tranquilizers, a variety of antihistamines, a few drops of antifreeze, and some grains of rat poison. The bowl is overflowing with a pasty powder. Marie saves two whole sheets for herself and then starts dicing the vegetables for the osso buco. It's a slightly sweet dish, ideal for diluting the taste of antifreeze and the cocktail of pills so Laurent doesn't notice them. Thomas will die very quickly. A few spoonfuls of stewed apple. The sound of the knife on the wooden chopping board reverberates around the room. Alone at the center of this drama, she knows she's making the right decision. Marie has rested her mother's recipe book facing her to be sure she doesn't forget a single step. The tomatoes are reducing slowly in a pan. The butter is starting to brown the pieces of meat in the large cast-iron casserole dish she so loves using. It's not a crime to take back what you yourself have brought into the world. Marie now has the opportunity to correct what she still sees as her own mistake. Soon this little family will no longer exist. Laurent will never have to suffer the truth. She's taking life back from life and no one will judge her.

⋮

The osso buco needs to simmer on very low heat for another hour. Marie has gone to pick up Thomas early from the day nursery. Laurent isn't home yet. All the mixtures are ready. She just needs to do everything in the right order. Thomas will be the first to go. His little body won't tolerate the combination in his stomach for more than three minutes. Marie thinks that it would be a serious mistake to give him his stewed apple before serving Laurent his food. The drugs will take longer to work on Laurent and he's bound to notice anything suspect in his son's behavior instantly. The scheme would fail. For Thomas's main couse, she's planned chicken and spinach—with no poison. He mustn't eat too much or he won't be hungry when it comes to dessert. The numbers are lining up, the proportions becoming clear, everything's calculated, measured, and quantified in her mind. Marie has always been methodical and thorough. When she threw herself into a project, she put infinite care into fine-tuning the tiniest details that no one else had even thought of.

Laurent calls. He tells her not to wait for him for dinner, he's very behind with his work. Marie tries to disguise her panic while still being firm with her husband: "Come on, I cooked for hours to make a nice meal for the three of us. I need this special time now. Thomas and I will wait for you till midnight if need be. But come home early for once. Please…" Marie knows the arguments that will persuade Laurent: abandoning his family, guilt for not spending enough time with his son, the dish that his wife lovingly prepared. Family forever.

Laurent was half lying to his wife. He's planning to have a drink with Julia after work. He needs to relax away from Marie and Thomas before getting the news from the lab or from Paul. His fears about the results of the test have been needling him for three days. He needs some courage to go home and sit with his family while he waits for the outcome of his own life as a man and a father.

Paul messages him to say he'll stop off at the lab at the end of the day to pick up the results in person and will let him know right away. Laurent feels relieved. He decides to go home early, maybe make the most of the last period of calm.

Marie is wearing the dress Laurent bought her for her last birthday. She had seen it in the window of a department store when they were strolling along the boulevard Haussmann with Thomas. It was a very cold day. Snow had cloaked the tops of cars and left a thick blackish slush on the sidewalks for people to squelch through. She remembers how happy she was when she opened the big gift-wrapped parcel. This gorgeous dress that he remembered for her. Marie couldn't bear to have all her memories wiped out, soiled, punctured by the appalling truth. She finds the thought of death more bearable. With this combination of drugs and poison, he'll go to sleep painlessly. He won't touch her again. It will be like a long family nap, so they can forget everything and meet up again somewhere else, somewhere far from excruciating reality.

It's six thirty when Marie hears the first sound in the lock. He's really made an effort. He's come home very early today to make the most of this family meal. The routine is still the same. The keys put on the small sideboard, the door still half open, the shoes on the floor, the coat hung on the hook on the right, the door slamming, Marie's name called toward the kitchen. It's the last time.

"Dinnertime!"

:

Today seemed to go on forever. As he closes the door to his office, Paul remembers his last conversation with his closest friend, Laurent. This evening, whatever the verdict, it will be up to him to tell Laurent the results of his paternity test. Interns are still running down corridors, laden with files. Salpêtrière hospital is one of the few places that never sleeps, open twenty-four hours a day, home to thousands of people every day: from medical students to the seriously ill, from specialists to mere observers, from doctors to researchers, all of them spread through the vast buildings on its campus. Paul remembers that at the start of his career he took months to identify the different floors in the gynecology department.

Now, though, he feels at home here. He could make the trip to the lab for Laurent's results with his eyes closed.

"Hi there, Guy, I need the results for test number 89097034." The fifty-something secretary types on his computer keyboard to find out where the results are. They're not here. The department has decided to transfer part of the laboratory into an annex, outside the gynecology department. Paul is irritated. He doesn't understand why doctors are always last to be given practical information.

It's eight forty-five. Paul has to retrace his steps and come out of the building to make his way to the west wing. He knows Laurent is waiting anxiously for these results. He's already annoyed with himself for being slightly late and thinks he should let him know by text. He searches his pockets and realizes he left his cell phone on his desk. He quickens his step along the hospital's corridors, not even taking the trouble to greet coworkers along the way. A young woman hands him the results of the test at last. He knows there's no possible room for doubt. He doesn't open it immediately, choosing instead to pick up his phone so he can call Laurent as soon as possible.

It's nine fifteen. The clocks in the hallway show the exact time, down to the last second. Paul is sweating. Anxious to know the verdict, he can feel his heart thudding in his chest. His heartbeat accelerates, his blood pressure rises, his hands are growing clammy and cold as they clutch that envelope. When he finally reaches his office, Paul grabs his phone. Laurent has called twice but left no message. Once at eight thirty and then again at eight forty-five.

Paul sits at his desk for a moment. He opens the envelope and unfolds the two sheets of paper. He doesn't take long to find his friend's phone number. He and Laurent call each other a lot. He calls him back. It rings several times with no reply. Paul tries again three times. Three calls go unanswered. He decides to leave a message: "Laurent, it's Paul. So I have the results. There's no doubt about it, the test is ninety-nine percent positive. You're definitely Thomas's father."